BAD ROYAL

CLARISSA WILD

Copyright © 2018 Clarissa Wild
All rights reserved.
ISBN: 9781081278762

© 2018 Clarissa Wild

This is a work of fiction. Names, characters, places and incidents are either the product of the author's imagination or are used fictitiously. Any resemblance to actual events, places, organizations, or person, whether living or dead, is entirely coincidental.

All rights reserved. No part of this book may be reproduced, transmitted in any form or by any means, electronic or mechanical, including photocopying, recording, or by any information storage retrieval system. Doing so would break licensing and copyright laws.

Chapter 1

AMIR

"As your advisor, I have to be honest with you, and right now ... I really think this is the worst idea you've come up with."

I laugh as I look at Hassan through the mirror while buttoning up the blue shirt he brought. Every time he asks me a question, I wonder why I even brought him along. "Of course, it is. That's why I'm doing it."

"But My Prince ..."

"Amir is fine, Hassan," I say as I have so many times before, but it never seems to stick. Although he's been my advisor for some time, he just can't get past the official terms for some reason.

"Amir," he says, "Do we really have to go through with

this?"

I adjust my shirt and tuck it into my white pants before zipping up. "Yes. I'm going. End of story."

There's no way I'm pulling out now. Not when I'm already cooped up in this hotel far away from the busy palace. I need this night. Just one night.

"But what if the press finds out?" Hassan says.

"They won't," I say as I turn to face him. "It's evening. The venue will be dark. Besides, I'm in disguise. It'll be fine. Did you bring the scarf I asked for?"

"Of course, Your Highness." He immediately fishes ten of them out of the oversized bag he brought. "Which color did you want? Size?" He holds them up as I contemplate.

"Red one," I say, pointing at it, but then I lower my finger. "Or do you think blue would suit this better?" I look myself up and down in the mirror, wondering if this'll work.

"That depends on what you're trying to achieve," he says.

"I want to look as normal as possible," I say, frowning as I check myself in the mirror. Will anyone notice it's me? I hope not. I'll have to think of an excuse if they do question me; otherwise, I'll just make a run for it. Simple.

"Normal …" Hassan clears his throat. "Well, you look outstanding to me, Your Royal Highness."

"So do I look like you?" I ask.

"Like me?" His lips part, confused. "Um … well, I guess."

"This is how you dress in your free time, right?" I ask, doing a twirl for him.

I'm only copying what I've seen him wear so many times.

"Yes, but ... it's not suited for a prince."

"No, Hassan. Remember what I said." I raise a brow at him.

He smashes his lips together and repeats what I told him like a parrot. "Right ... You're not a prince tonight."

I wink. "Exactly."

"Let's just hope everyone else thinks that way too, or we'll be in a world of trouble."

I pat his shoulder, laughing. "It'll be fine. Don't worry about that."

Even if I do get into trouble, I won't drag him into it. That's a promise I intend to keep.

I snatch the scarf from his hand and tie it around my neck.

"You always say that, yet things have always ended badly."

"When? Where?"

"When your father finds out," he says with a load of snark.

"He won't find out this time, trust me," I say. "And if, for some reason, someone does find out, I promise I won't even mention your name. Your job is safe. I promise."

"Thank you, My Prince. But if anyone recognizes you—"

"With this disguise?" I interject as I turn to face him, complete with a set of tinted glasses. "Nah, I don't think so."

"You look ..."

"Dashing?"

"Well, I wouldn't say that." He folds his arms. "It's so unbecoming for royalty."

I grin. "Precisely what I was aiming for."

"But you're wearing the scarf around your neck," he says. "Why not around your head?"

"Because that's how I always wear it. People don't even know what the top of my head looks like." I shrug. "If I go out like this, I might get away with just being me."

"I doubt it," Hassan says, making me sigh.

"I just want to have a bit of fun, okay?" I say. "Just don't tell my father."

"Yes, yes, of course, I won't. You have my word."

"Thanks," I say, winking as I shove a bill into his hand. "And do something fun for yourself too tonight."

"Is this …? Are you buying my loyalty, Your Highness?" He attempts to shove the bill back into my hand, but I won't allow it.

"No, Hassan. I'm just saying I want you to chill. Relax. Get out. Do something fun. Find a girl. Hook up. Go crazy."

"Crazy? But you know that's not—"

"Anything is allowed tonight," I say as I turn around and grab my keys. "No rules. No judgment. End of story."

He stays put in the middle of the room, looking a bit befuddled. "Wait. You're going? Are you sure?"

"Yes. Now. And don't even think about following me," I say, before closing the door behind me.

***

Adrenaline surges through my body as I make my way through the crowded streets, clutching my scarf close to my lips, hoping no one will recognize me. I get the few odd stares every now and then, but by the time they turn to look again, I've already disappeared into the sea of people.

I love the thrill of going out in public like this, not knowing when or if someone will recognize me and scream my name from the top of their lungs. The danger excites me, making me do these sorts of things even when I know I'm not supposed to.

My father's rules won't stop me from chasing my needs, though. On the contrary, they only push me further into the limelight and further away from him and all the responsibilities that come with being the son of the king.

I'm trying to blend in when I finally spot the place I'm looking for. River NightClub. One of the few places in this city where men and women flock together without shame. It's normally chock-full of tourists, and I sneak inside, pretending to be one of them.

The music is blaring, and I'm already in love with what I see. People dancing, drinking, fondling each other, or even kissing in full view. If Father saw this, he'd be out of his mind. Not that he'd ever come into a place like this.

He considers it forbidden. Out of the question. He only tolerates these businesses because they make him a lot of money, which is hypocritical, if you ask me, but I don't mind. It allows me to have a fun night out without being tied to any royal obligations.

And boy, am I enjoying myself thoroughly … watching that girl dancing on her own in the far corner of the club. Her blond hair waving back and forth as she sways her voluptuous hips. Her skintight black dress a stark contrast to her pearly white skin, but mesmerizing nonetheless. And those pristine blue eyes that latch onto mine as I approach her seal the deal.

A smirk spreads on my lips. I wonder if she's here for a purpose too. If she's looking at me because she finds it just as hard to look away. If she likes what she sees.

Because I sure do.

I didn't just come here to dance or drink or mingle.

I came here to find someone to spend the night with.

And I think I just found the perfect girl to play pretend with.

Lord, have mercy on my soul, because I'm about to sin.

Chapter 2

Maya

I tiptoe around on the music, trying to find my bearings, but the longer I do, the more I'm beginning to question why I even came to this club. Or why I even listened to my cousin Lesley when she told me to step outside my comfort zone and take a leap of faith. God, this is so unlike me. Questioning everything as though I'm in the middle of some sort of fucking identity crisis.

I'm not. I came to this country of my own free will.

I came because I wanted to do something different.

Because I dared to apply for a job halfway across the world, thinking I wouldn't get it. But I did it anyway, with a tiny push from Lesley. She always has the best ideas. It's true, because this whole place is magical.

I shouldn't waste time feeling sad because I'm alone and literally know no one here. I should have fun, for crying out loud. That's why I came here tonight anyway. I can sip drinks at the hotel too, but this place actually plays good music.

So fuck this emotional bullshit. Fuck this insecurity. I'm gonna do it.

In a bout of energetic enthusiasm, I walk away from the bar and find a small place to myself in the corner of the club where I can dance to my heart's content. I close my eyes and let my body do what it does best. I turn off my brain and focus on the here and now. The sound of the beat drops so low I can feel it in my toes. I love it so much that I can't help but let go in the moment, ignoring anyone and everything around me. I don't give a shit what anyone thinks of the way I'm dancing, or that I'm alone in a foreign country, dancing in some strange club with people who don't speak the same language as I do.

I dared myself to do this, and now I'm going for it.

With my drink still in my hand, I sway to the music, ignoring the voice in my head telling me it could be dangerous. Because who knows what could happen when you're abroad and all alone. But I refuse to live in fear. Instead, I'll enjoy every second of my time here while it lasts.

And when I open my eyes ... I come face to face with heaven.

Well, that's what it feels like anyway when two pristine blue eyes stare right back at me and take my breath away. A guy in an all-white outfit in the far corner of this club has caught my attention, and I can't look away. Part of his face is hidden behind a scarf, but it doesn't make him any less mesmerizing. I'm completely frozen to the ground as he walks in my direction.

Is he really coming toward me? Or am I dreaming?

I clutch my drink, but my legs are shaking as the man approaches me. Should I stay put and see what happens? Or run away and never come back? What if he's here to kidnap me?

Don't be ridiculous. No one's going to kidnap you in the middle of a club with hundreds of people around.

But then why is he looking at me like that? Like he just … found exactly what he's looking for?

I'm locked in indecision until there's no way to back out.

He's right in front of me now. His eyes still on mine like a hawk honing in on its prey. Slowly, he peruses my body, taking in every detail and making me feel stripped naked.

With two fingers, he tugs down the scarf around his lips. The smirk that appears underneath makes my heart beat in my throat.

He's gorgeous. Drop-dead gorgeous.

I swallow away the lump in my throat as he grabs my drink from my hand and places it on the small table behind me, then grabs my hand. The touch of his skin against mine sends delicious shocks throughout my body, and my brain turns to mush as he drags me farther onto the dance floor.

The music is loud and silences the noise in my head as this stranger dances with me. His moves are sexy and downright dirty, but not too filthy. Just the right amount to keep me hooked. I don't know what I'm doing or why; I just know I don't want it to stop.

I've never been the kind of girl to just dance with a

random stranger, but this guy ... he's something else. An invisible attraction exists between us that neither of us can fight, and I don't even want to.

I just want him to swoop me up and take me out of here.

It's silly and totally irresponsible and dangerous, but I'm thinking it anyway.

Maybe being in a foreign country does things to your brain that makes you want crazy things.

Or maybe it's just this guy who does the trick for me.

Because holy hell, I can't keep my eyes off him, he's that hot. Light blue eyes that light me on fire when I look at them. Short, tousled black hair, a little curly on the ends. A hint of scruff around his firm jawline. Muscles peeking out from underneath his shirt. Thick lips showing a grin with just the right amount of arrogance.

It's as though he just walked out of my dreams.

We're getting closer and closer. I'm lost in the music, lost in his eyes. His hands are on my body, holding my waist and pulling me close as we dance to the rhythm. And as my eyes slowly close more and more, I do the craziest thing.

I let this stranger kiss me.

Full on the lips.

And fuck me ... does it feel good.

His kiss numbs the voices in my head telling me not to do stupid things. It's so good that I can't even stop kissing him back.

His lips part and his tongue dips out to lick mine, but only for a quick taste, nothing more. He's giving me a sample of what he's got to offer ... and boy, do I want more.

My arms wrap around his neck as his hands snake around my waist. We're locked in a sensuous greed neither of us wants to escape. And I don't even know why.

I never do this. I never go out without friends, and I certainly never kiss strangers like this. And I don't even know his name.

For a few seconds, I come to my senses, and my lips unlatch from his. But I can still taste him on my tongue … and holy shit, does it taste good.

But I have to keep my focus to stop from going too far. At least, that's what I tell myself because Lord, this man will make it hard. So hard.

He seems just as struck by our sudden desire to kiss as he blinks a couple of times and remains frozen on the floor.

Then his lips crash right back onto mine, breaking every train of thought I had. My brain feels as though it's turning into mush as he plants one delicious kiss after another. I'm helpless to fight it, and the more his hands slide across my body, the more turned on I get. The heat of the dance floor and the beat of the music only add to the delirium, and I'm finding it hard to think about anything other than jumping this man's bones.

It's wrong, it's so wrong, but the longer our mouths are locked, the more I'm beginning to lose my senses. He's guiding me away from the floor and into the bathroom, all while kissing me senseless. And I don't even mind as long as he doesn't stop.

We're lucky no one's around because the moment we burst through the door, he's got his hands all over my body, groping me in places that make me all hot and bothered. He groans into my mouth as he whisks me off the ground and sets me on the bathroom counter. He positions himself between my thighs and holds me down while kissing me hard and fast. It's all going so quickly, I feel like I'm stuck in a whirlwind of excitement, and I don't want it to stop. Even though it's so damn wrong, and I'm out of my mind for letting this stranger touch me like this. But fuck me, he knows just what buttons to push to make me say yes to pretty much anything, including being fucked right here in the bathroom of some foreign club.

His lips are everywhere—on my neck, my cheeks, my collarbone. Even his tongue comes out to play. Drawing lines everywhere, he's toying with my tongue and licking the roof of my mouth. He nibbles on my bottom lip until I moan, and when our eyes briefly lock, I lose every inch of control.

"Have you ever been fucked by a stranger?" he murmurs against my skin as his fingers dive between my legs. He's touching me right there underneath my black dress. He's fondling me in public, grazing my pussy with his fingers, and worst of all … I don't want it to stop.

I shake my head and realize I'm about to make a dumb decision. But I can't help myself. Not with him. I've never done anything this dangerously stupid with a random guy I just met, but he's not just any guy. This man … he's something else.

He knows just how to touch me to make me want to beg for more. Especially when he starts toying with my pussy right through the fabric of my panties.

A hot breath of air leaves my mouth as I tilt my head back while his mouth leaves delicious pecks on my skin. I struggle to breathe as he plays with me, pushing me closer and closer to the edge.

That's when he grabs my thighs and pulls me off the bathroom counter, only to turn me around and push me face down against it. Grunting, he hooks his fingers around my panties and tears them off. Within seconds, a packet is ripped, and I hear a zipper come undone. I gaze at him through the mirror as he grips my ass and positions himself behind me.

The moment his tip enters me, I gasp. He's huge, and the farther he thrusts, the more I feel as though I'm about to explode. Fuck.

I'm being fucked by a stranger, and I'm loving it. There's nothing more wrong, more illicit than this, yet I can't bring myself to end it. It feels so good, making my eyes roll into the back of my head. That's how hard he's banging me against the counter.

I can feel myself come undone from the sheer force of his thrusts, and I moan out loud. His dick pulsates inside me, amplifying the pleasure as we both come at the same time, moaning like animals.

When my orgasm subsides, he pulls out and takes off the condom, tying it up and throwing it in the trash. Before I've even had a chance to look at him, he's already zipped himself up again as if nothing ever happened.

As I get up, he takes ahold of my body again and pulls me in for a toe-curling kiss. One I won't forget anytime soon.

"What's your name?" he asks, his voice dark and sultry.

"Maya," I reply, my throat clamping up.

"Maya …" He licks his top lip in a way that makes me feel as if he just laid claim to my name. "Amir." He grabs my hand and presses a kiss on top. What a gentleman.

My brain is still trying to process what happened when someone suddenly enters the bathroom, and my entire face flushes.

"Ahh ..." the woman mumbles, gazing at both of us.

I clear my throat and quickly pull down my dress. "Sorry, I was just ... washing out my clothes," I lie as I try to hide the panties underneath the sink.

She glances back and forth at both of us as a wicked smile appears on her lips. Of course, she caught us kissing. I just pray she didn't see anything else.

"Excuse me," she says as she tries to pass us both. However, she stops midway, and her eyes remain fixated on Amir. "Hey ... you look like ... aren't you—"

"No, I'm not," Amir interrupts with a strict tone, and he quickly pulls his scarf back over his lips.

The woman flinches and makes a face. Then she goes into a cubicle but not before throwing a final glare our way. Who was she? Or more importantly ... why does she know him?

But before I can ask him, he's already gone.

Disappeared through the door as though he never even existed.

Chapter 3

AMIR

I drop onto my bed and stare at the ceiling, breathing out a sigh. Fuck me. That was insane. But worth it, nonetheless.

God, that girl ... those lips ... and that fuck.

Even though it's been an hour since I last saw her, I can still taste her sweet lips and feel her pussy on my dick. I wish I could've kissed her a little longer. And maybe fingered her too. I would've brought her back to this hotel room for a second round if that woman hadn't interrupted us.

Why did she have to recognize me?

I close my eyes and try not to think about it, but the image of that girl continues to spring into my mind. She was beautiful. So fucking beautiful. Not like the girls from here. I rarely see them with that kind of pearly white hair and almost translucent skin. It was mesmerizing. And the way she danced? Fuck me, it made me want to rip off her clothes and lick her body. So I did.

I normally never just randomly fuck them and especially not in a bathroom, for fuck's sake. But I couldn't stop myself. The moment my lips crashed into hers, I needed to have her, had to claim her for my own then and there.

I cover my face with both hands because just thinking about the way I fucked her against the bathroom counter causes my pants to tighten from my growing cock.

Why am I even thinking about this? I'll probably never see her again. But why does that piss me off so much? Damn.

***

Maya

Even though it's already morning, I can't stop thinking about last night.

I can't believe I had sex with a man and only learned his name afterward. God, this is so unlike me. I don't usually kiss on the first date, let alone let a man screw me like that.

But he ... he was something else, that's for sure.

While I'm sipping coffee and enjoying breakfast here at the hotel, the memory of our kiss and fuck keeps a constant smile on my face. I'm normally never this easy, but this encounter has left me giddy. Maybe I should let go more often.

This trip has only been amazing so far. I've seen huge skyscrapers in the middle of the desert and rode camels to some unknown oasis. And the people here are so different from what I'm used to as well—very calm and collected unlike back home where everything's so noisy. I've gotten so used to New York's bustling sounds that I've forgotten what nice and quiet sounds like ... and here in Dakai, I'm rediscovering that peace.

The place isn't all progressive, though. We're not technically allowed to go all bananas in public, wear skimpy clothes, or touch in public, let alone kiss. Or fuck.

Jesus, I really did break a couple of laws. I hope I won't get thrown into jail. Here's to hoping the woman couldn't identify me.

Not that I've seen anyone get arrested yet, so I assume the authorities aren't on it like hawks. Maybe they're lenient. Besides, kissing and touching is allowed in the clubs, though what we did definitely broke all the rules.

Goddamn, I'm smirking to myself again just thinking about that stranger ... *Amir.* His name alone makes the goose bumps appear on my skin again. He was too sexy to be true, and sometimes I still wonder if it all really happened.

Not that it'll ever happen again. I don't know where he lives or what his last name is, so I'll probably never see him again. Still, a girl can hope, right?

But I have to remember I'm not here to hook up. I have business to attend to today. I was invited to this country to design clothing for the royal family, and when I found out they'd picked me for the job, I completely freaked out. I didn't expect to actually get it, let alone be designing for royalty.

But here I am, and I'm making my parents as well as myself proud.

After finishing breakfast, I hurry out the hotel to go to my appointment. My contact isn't directly with the royal family, of course; it's with one of their many assistants, as expected. Hell, I don't think I'll ever even meet any of them. But it's humbling to know they're going to wear what I create. It's not every day you get to work for royals, so I'll do my utmost best.

I take a taxi to the square in front of the palace. I'm glued to the window because I can't take my eyes off the beautiful architecture. Especially the palace … wow. It's brilliant white with luscious plants growing on all sides, potted plants as huge as a one-story building, big black doors, and ancient looking statues.

The taxi guy drops me off right in front of the square as he's not allowed to go any farther. Luckily, I know where to go.

After paying him, I walk through the middle of the square, passing all the tourists. A few big cars are parked out near the end of the street—probably some rich people showing off. I know for sure when I see a guy wearing a long white garment and a black headband around his head leaning back with his elbows against the hood of his car, flaunting two girls at his side. But my jaw drops the moment I realize who it is.

Amir.

I stop in my tracks and stare for a few seconds, wondering if I'm dreaming.

But then he laughs, and I can hear his voice. It's definitely him.

He's really here. What are the odds?

And at that moment, he suddenly turns his head and stares right back at me.

The moment seems to last forever, and I can't look away.

I know he's seen me, but does he recognize me? Does he remember the girl he fucked in the bathroom of a dance club?

I swallow when I see one of the girls placing a peck on his cheeks, and my mood immediately sours. Of course, he'd be that kind of guy. Kissing random girls you've never met, banging them whenever he can. Why would I expect anything less? He probably doesn't even remember my face, let alone my name. I should've known better than to just let myself go with the first guy who showed interest in me.

I shake my head and turn away, determined not to let this sway me from my goal. I'm not here to find a boyfriend or have casual sex. I'm here to do my job. To make kickass clothes and make a name for myself. To put my brand on the map and become a famous designer. That's what's important right now.

So I keep my head high and walk on ahead to the palace. The side entrance is where I'm supposed to enter. The assistant told me someone will open the door for me, so I'm assuming they know I'm coming.

When I get to the gate, I ring the doorbell and wait for an answer. "Business inquiries only," a stern voice says.

"I'm here for an appointment with Mrs. Adallah. She said you knew I was coming."

A few minutes pass before someone comes strolling to the gate to unlock it manually. Guess they really don't like to let people in. Or maybe they wanna check if it's really me.

"Passport please," the man says before he allows me in.

I reluctantly pull it out and show it to him. His eyes scan the pages before he gives it back. "All right. C'mon."

By the time I've put my passport back in my bag, the man's already gone ahead. I have trouble keeping up with him without looking like I'm rushing, but I don't want to make a fool out of myself because I'm about to meet someone who actually works for royalty.

When we're close to the entrance, the man suddenly takes my bag and puts it under an X-ray machine, probably to check if I brought anything dangerous. I guess you can't be too careful with royalty and stuff. Luckily, I pass the test.

My heart's beating out of my chest when he opens a door and beckons for me to enter. My eyes are peeled as I marvel at the beauty inside. White marble slabs line the floors and walls, the décor extravagant because of the gold practically slathered on everything. Gold fountains, gold lining along the pillars in the middle, golden statues, and even flaky golden pots filled with plants and flowers.

"Last door on your left. Do not go anywhere else. It is forbidden," the man barks.

Before I can reply, the door has already shut, and I feel as though I've been trapped in the most beautiful prison in the world. I'm not even sure I'd be mad if they forced me to stay.

I tiptoe around and try to gape at the massive halls, but every time someone passes, I feel like a peeping Tom crossing boundaries I shouldn't cross. So I opt for the safe route and immediately go to my left.

When I'm at the last door, I clear my throat and knock on the door.

A woman in a few layers of colorful fabric opens the door, and I part my lips, a little unsure of what to say. "Hi. I'm the new designer. I'm supposed to meet with Mrs. Adallah today."

"You're Maya?" the woman says, her sparkling eyes lighting up. "It's so nice to meet you." She shakes my hand and opens the door even farther, pulling me inside as she begins to talk. "Come in, come in."

We sit down in her office, where she offers me a cup of tea and explains to me what I'll be doing. It's standard practice, and nothing I've never heard before. The whole conversation takes an hour maybe, tops. When all is said and done, and the contract is signed, I know exactly what's expected of me, including the fact I'm to remain silent about this to the press until after the clothing I've made has been worn. Any private business I witness is also not to be discussed, which is completely understandable. I mean, it's the palace, after all, and I'm sure the media are as hungry for news and gossip here as they are back in the States.

But I don't mind. The pay is great, and I get to do what I love. They're giving me free rein on the fabrics and anything else I need. Nothing is too expensive, which is like a designer's dream come true.

By the time we've gone through it all, I'm giddy to get started. When we get up, she says, "Okay then. Let me introduce you to your client."

Mrs. Adallah walks me through the corridors and up a flight of stairs. Then through what feels like endless halls alongside beautiful gardens until we stop at a huge door with a guard standing on each side.

I clutch my bag close to my body and bite the inside of my cheek, wondering who's going to be wearing the clothes I make. If it's a man or a woman, what their status is, their size … all of it changes what clothes I need to make.

"Is he ready?" Mrs. Adallah asks the guards.

One of them knocks on the door, and yells, "Your visitors have arrived."

There's a voice that echoes behind it. "Come in."

The guards step aside, and Mrs. Adallah opens the door, hesitantly stepping inside. I follow her, but I can't see a thing other than her back while she speaks up.

"Your Highness? Are you ready?"

Your Highness? What?

I'm stunned, and even though I open my mouth, nothing rolls off my tongue except soft mumbles. I'm going to actually design clothes for a royal?

"It's time for your appointment with the designer," Mrs. Adallah says. "She's here to take your measurements and talk through a couple of ideas."

She grabs my arm and pulls me forward into the room.

My eyes are immediately drawn toward a man sitting in a giant square bath, naked.

Females around him pour water on him, washing him.

And when he turns his head, all the blood drains from my face.

Amir.

Chapter 4

AMIR

The moment our eyes lock, my whole body goes cold, despite the fact I'm in a scorching hot bath. It's her. The girl from the club. And from the looks of it, she's noticed it's me too.

Fuck.

What is she doing here?

One of the women tries to rub my skin with a washcloth, but I push her away. "Not now."

"Sorry, Your Highness," she says, backing away.

"Bath time is over," I tell the women, who immediately leave, still wearing their bikinis. They'll dress somewhere else, as always.

I wasn't expecting Mrs. Adallah to come in with

company. And that it'd be … *Maya*.

"Maya?" I mumble, still shocked about seeing her in the flesh.

Her eyes widen, and her face turns strawberry red, so I'm guessing it really is her. Wow. What a coincidence. And here I thought I wouldn't ever see her again.

"Your Highness?" Mrs. Adallah says, raising her brow. "It's time for your appointment with the designer, remember?"

"*She's* the designer?" I ask, my brows drawing together. When neither of them responds, I burst out into laughter. "Well, isn't that a coincidence."

"Do you two … know each other?" Mrs. Adallah asks, her eyes shifting back and forth between me and Maya.

"Oh, yes," I say, biting my lip, thinking about all the kisses we shared … and the way I banged her against the bathroom counter.

God, I was planning to do so much more to that beautiful girl. I wanted to take her back to my hotel room and lick her entire body before claiming it again and again. Too bad someone recognized me, forcing me to leave before anyone else found out.

When the silence becomes awkward, Mrs. Adallah places a few documents on my desk and smiles. "Well … I'll leave you two to it then," Mrs. Adallah says, then she turns around and leaves.

Maya stays put right in front of the door, her body practically frozen to the ground.

I don't blame her. Discovering the guy you fucked at a local club is the actual prince must be hard to swallow. Not as hard as something else I would've made her swallow … if

I'd had the chance.

I rub my chin. I might still get that chance after all.

I step out of the floor bathtub, and her eyes immediately follow down toward my V-line, and probably beyond.

"Towel," she mutters, shutting her eyes.

I look down and laugh. Crap. I completely forgot I'm naked.

I quickly grab a towel, and say, "Sorry."

"Jesus …" she adds, making me laugh even more.

It's not like she hasn't had it inside her before. She just hadn't seen me yet because I fucked her so fast and immediately zipped up afterward. I smirk. Well, she has now.

With my towel curled around my waist, I dry myself off with another one and then saunter off toward my closet. "It's safe to look now," I say, wondering if she's thinking about my cock.

"Right," she says sarcastically. "Why do I find that hard to believe?"

She sure has sass. "I promise I won't moon you."

"But you couldn't wait to show me your dick," she scoffs. As if she's actually mad.

"Hey now," I say, putting on some underwear and pants. "That was a mistake."

"Really? You forgot you were naked? In bath? With a bunch of … girls?"

I laugh again. "For the record, those are professional washing ladies."

She cringes. "TMI, Amir. TMI."

"What? Jealous?" I raise a brow. Maybe she has thought about me.

Her face scrunches up. "You wish."

Oh, so feisty. I love it. Still, I get that she may have been offended by what she saw. Finding out the random guy you fucked is a prince, and then discovering him in the tub with his washing ladies probably isn't a great memory to add to the collection.

"I apologize for the way this introduction has gone," I say. "But let me make it up to you."

I put on a purple shirt and close my closet, walking toward her. "I'm ready for whatever you need me to do."

She slowly opens her eyes, revealing those beautiful irises again that continue to draw in my complete attention. "As long as you're not naked."

"Oh c'mon, I'm sure you liked what you saw. Besides, it's not as if you didn't like it when I gave it to you," I jest, taking a long sketchbook from her hand. "What's this?"

She tries to snatch it back from me, but I turn away and walk toward my desk.

"Those are my drawings," she says, approaching me. "Give that back, please."

I open it and flip through pages and pages of beautiful sketches and outlines of amazing dresses, skirts, tops, pants, and pretty much anything else you can wear.

Suddenly, her fast fingers grasp it, and she takes it away from me. "Those are personal."

"They're amazing," I say. "Love it."

She blushes again. It looks good on her. So good, it makes me want to keep pushing her, so I can see those red cheeks again and again.

"Thanks, I guess." She swallows when I catch her looking at me, and then she immediately looks away.

"Anyway, let's get started then."

"Right … because that's what you're here for. To design clothes." I clear my throat as I sit down behind my desk. "I didn't know you were the one they hired."

"As if *I* knew."

"What do you mean?" I ask, frowning.

"No one told me I'd be working directly for the royals," she says.

"Really? I'm surprised it wasn't mentioned," I reply.

"They only said I'd be working in the palace."

Interesting. I'll definitely have to speak to Mrs. Adallah about that.

I point at the chair in front of the desk, and say, "Sit, sit."

She grabs the chair, slowly turns it, and carefully sits down as if she's afraid to break the thing or something. That, or her ass is made of porcelain. Honestly, it makes me want to laugh.

"What? What's so funny?" she asks.

"Nothing," I say. "It's just so extraordinary …" I gaze up at her from under my eyelashes. "To see you again."

She licks her lips, and for some reason, I imagine it's me licking them instead. "It was quite a surprise to me too, actually." She makes a face. "Especially with the whole … bathing scene."

"Oh, yeah, I'm sorry. If I'd known Mrs. Adallah was going to immediately let you in, I would've been dressed already."

"Hmm … right." She gazes down at her sketchbook, almost as if she's thinking about something else right now. I wonder what's on her mind.

"Is that ... Those women ..." Her lips are still parted, but she doesn't finish her sentence. "Never mind."

I smile, and say, "You mean the ladies who washed me? That's normal, yes."

She nods, clearly confused. "Right ... Because you're a royal and all."

"Exactly." Why do I get the feeling they don't do that where she's from?

And why, when I look into her eyes, do I sense a slight hint of jealousy?

"If you're curious, I don't do anything with them. Physically. They just wash me. That's it."

"I didn't ask." Her voice is blunt, almost as if she's embarrassed.

"But you wanted to know, so now you have the answer," I reply with a grin.

She seems even angrier now, and I love how it looks on her.

"No, I was just confused, that's all," she says, clearing her throat. "Anyway, let's begin."

Chapter 5

Maya

I don't think anything as remotely uncomfortable as this has happened in my life.

Like catching him while he's naked. Watching a bunch of girls bathe him.

Not to mention the fact this is the same dude I hooked up with at the club mere hours ago.

I'm starting to wonder if I should doubt my sanity right now. I mean, if this isn't otherworldly, I don't know what is.

Especially the women touching him like that, both outside the palace and in the bath … it gave me the itches. Made me want to rinse myself off and tear my hair out. But why? Why am I so upset when I don't even know this man? At least not beyond the quick kiss and fuck we shared.

Part of me feels a little deceived because he could've told me he was the prince before he hooked up with me. Though, I'm not even sure whether that would've stopped me from jumping his bones. Because damn ... was I horny last night.

Still, I can't help but feel a bit begrudged over what I just witnessed. And not just that, but how the hell did this guy go from flaunting his expensive car outside the palace to taking a nude bath with a bunch of women? Apparently, my conversation with Mrs. Adallah took a lot of time. There's no other explanation.

That, or I'm losing my mind.

I try not to make it awkward as I run my ribbon around his waist and chest, determining the sizes I need. Even though I'm sweating profusely just from being so close to him, I refuse to acknowledge any effect he may have on me.

When I catch him staring at me as I come around to the front, my entire face turns warm. A sinful grin spreads on his lips that reminds me of last night. And what I saw when he came out of that deep floor tub ... a long, juicy, dangling cock.

God. I didn't even see his dick at the club. It had all happened so fast. One moment, we were kissing, and the next, I was bent over the counter being fucked in the pussy. I loved how it felt, and I knew he was big.

I just didn't know he was *that* big.

Fuck.

I look away and sigh. Why can't I get these images out of my mind?

He's the prince, for God's sake. He's unattainable. And an ass, judging by the way he dismisses girls as though they're disposable. Plus, he ditched me at the club without any explanation whatsoever. He could've said he had important business to attend to. Or lied. Whatever. Anything would've been better than how he just vanished.

"So ... you're an expat then?" he suddenly asks, probably trying to break the ice.

I roll up the tape and place it on the table. "I'm just here temporarily for business purposes."

"Right ..." He licks his lips as I hold up a few patches of fabric I brought to see which one matches his skin.

"So do you dress royalty often?"

"No. This is a once-in-a-lifetime thing," I reply.

His frown intensifies. "That'd be a shame."

"Why?" I ask, then shove the fabric that looks good into his hand. "Hold this, please."

"Because you'd probably make a lot of royalty happy with your designs."

I pause as his words repeat in my head. Did he just give me a compliment?

"Your drawings are very good," he adds.

"Thanks," I say, grabbing more fabrics to pair with it.

"I mean it," he says.

I pause again and take a deep breath. "Okay, what's this about?"

He shrugs. "Nothing. I'm just saying the truth."

I raise a brow. "Right. Why do I get the feeling you're trying to make me feel good?"

He flinches. "Would that make things all right between us?"

I step back and place both fabrics on the table. My lips part, but I find it hard to form the words I need. What in

God's name does he want me to say to that? So instead of replying, I grab my sketchbook and start sketching his figure so I can work on some designs. At least those aren't ambiguous.

"Is that normal in your country?" he asks.

"What?" I ask, quickly penciling him down.

"Not answering a question a prince asks you."

I bite the inside of my cheek, trying not to get angry, but boy, does this guy piss me off.

"Where I come from, there are no princes. Or kings, for that matter."

"USA, right?" he asks. "President then."

"He's still a person, just like I am. I don't have to answer him when I don't want to."

"Interesting …" He mulls it over for a few seconds as I continue drawing. "So you really aren't afraid to speak your mind around here?"

I cock my head. "No. Unless it can get me thrown into jail, then yes." I cross my legs as his eyes dip down and go over my body as though he wants to ravish it. "Is that what you're aiming for? Please, let me know now, so I can get out of here in time."

He smiles. "No, of course not. I would never," he says. "Besides, you're way too cute for jail."

I roll my eyes. "Don't try to woo me; it won't work."

"Who says I am?" He cheekily raises his brow, but then follows it with a wink, embarrassing me even more.

"This is strictly business," I say, pointing at my work.

"Of course, it is …"

Why do I get the sense he's not being serious at all right now?

I sigh. "Look, if you wanna do this another time, we—"

"No, no. Now is good. Now is perfect. I like this." He glances at me awkwardly. "Should I stay still?"

"Yes, please. I'm trying to finish the drawing."

"What comes after that?"

"I buy fabrics. I create the clothes. I give them to Mrs. Adallah."

He looks taken aback. "Wait. Are you telling me this is the only time I'm seeing you?"

"According to the terms laid out in this contract, yes." I point at the document on the desk.

"I didn't agree to that," he says, losing posture to read the fine print. "I'll have to speak with Mrs. Adallah about this."

I lean back and stare at him, confused. "Why?"

"Because I want to see you again, of course." He grins. "Why else?"

I don't even know what to do with that statement. But my body does because it goes from hot to cold, then back to hot in a flash.

I don't know why, but I have the sudden urge to flee, so I do. I grab all my things and attempt to put them away, but the moment I reach for the contract, he grabs my wrist instead.

"Wait. Don't go." He glances at my wrist, then immediately releases me when he realizes he's keeping me locked in place. "Sorry, I just …" He runs his fingers through his hair. "I wanted to apologize for the way I left you alone at the club. It was just that someone almost recognized me, and I didn't want to risk it. The press is always following me everywhere."

I nod. "It's okay. I wouldn't have done anything with you if I'd known you were royalty." That's probably a lie, but admitting the truth could get me in a world of trouble I don't wanna be in right now.

He makes a face. "Really? Because I could've sworn you were enjoying yourself thoroughly in the bathroom ... and that you're still angry I left you hanging." He comes closer. So close, I can smell his intoxicating cologne. The same cologne he wore that night at the club. The memories of our lips and bodies melding together come rushing back. And oh boy, what I wouldn't give for another kiss ... and for his cock to fill me up again. But that would be wrong ... so wrong.

He's the prince, and I'm his designer. It's forbidden. Explicitly. It says so right in the contract. I'm not supposed to enter into a relationship with any royal whatsoever. Just work-related talk, and that's it.

I swallow away the lump in my throat. "I'm not angry."

"Of course, you aren't," he says with a smug smile. "But I still wanted you to know that I'm sorry for leaving so abruptly, and that I intend to make it up to you." He grabs my hand and kisses the top. "Miss Maya."

I quickly pull my hand back because it feels too good to say no. But I should. I definitely should, considering I could go to jail for this. Also, he's a fucking prince. A dozen girls are lined up outside, waiting for him to pick one of them.

Why would he be interested in me?

I'm probably just another one of his conquests. A girl he fucked, another one to add to his collection. Once was enough. I'm not willing to be a part of his ego trip.

"Why?" I ask, holding my things close to me as if they'd

provide any sort of protection against the seductiveness that embodies him. Just the way he presents himself, oozing with sex, makes my legs shake. But I can't give in. Not again. Not now that I know who he really is.

"Because I like you," he says as I tread backward toward the door. "And I think you like me too."

Somehow, seemingly out of nowhere, the image of his huge dick flashes through my mind, and for a second there, I wonder how much more pleasure it could give me.

I can't think of this. Not now. Not again.

I shake my head. "Just because I was interested at the club doesn't mean I am now."

"Really?" he muses with a tempting half-smile. "I beg to differ. I saw you looking at me when I stepped out of the tub."

"There was hardly any other place to look," I retort. "And you made it incredibly hard to look away with that entrance."

"Or maybe you're just finding it really hard not to think about me …"

I bump into the door, and he places his hands right beside me against the wood, trapping me inside.

I'm stammering. "If I'd known at the club I was meeting you today, I wouldn't have ever—"

He places a finger on my lips. "I don't believe that."

"It's the truth," I say through gritted teeth as if that makes it any bit more believable.

He smirks. "Hmm …" Then he pulls away from the door.

I can breathe again. But I'm not sure how I feel about that because it's suddenly oddly empty around me.

"You're the first to say that," he says.

I snort. "Sounds like a lie. Girls are waiting in line for you. I saw them kiss you outside near your car."

"No, they're standing in line for the *prince*," he says, settling his direct gaze on me. "But you weren't. You didn't even know it was me."

I suck in a breath, unsure of what to say.

I'm not sure what any of this means. This moment. Our meeting. The way everything went. And by God … the chances of it all happening.

So I say the only thing that makes sense right now. My only sense of security in a foreign country where I know nothing of the people, the customs, or the dangers that come with having fucked the prince.

"It was a one-time thing only," I reply, opening the door.

Right before I leave, he says, "Pity. I would've loved a second try."

But the door's already closed behind me, and with it, my dignity has left the room as well.

Why? Because I'm still thinking about how badly I wanted him to kiss and fuck me again too.

Shit.

Chapter 6

Maya

The royals have given me an actual workshop to create all my designs. I'm flabbergasted at how generous they are, but then again, nothing's too extravagant when it comes to royals. I found that out the moment Amir told me professionally hired ladies wash him.

Not that I could ever complain. This workshop is literally all I could ever ask for. My place back home isn't this large. Plus, the closets are full of all the tools I need and more giant tables to work at, several mannequins, and different sewing machines. And best of all, I've got the place all to myself. It's a literal dream come true.

So I've spent the entire morning drawing out some designs, and now it's time to go shopping for fabrics. I mean, they do have some lying around here, but I need more, and Mrs. Adallah said I could spend as much as I wanted. They even gave me a credit card to use, which made my creative soul want to squeal.

When I'm done, I put all my sketches and pencils in my bag and go outside, locking the doors behind me. This damn heat makes me feel like I'm being bombarded by the sun, but after a while, I get used to the blistering heat. The city is bustling with people and vehicles, so it's tough trying to get through the crowd, but it's a rich experience nonetheless. It reminds me of New York; so much traffic in one place makes you feel like an ant.

I go to the market where I find stalls selling all sorts of things. Food, jewelry, clothing, bags, dishware, anything. You name it, they have it. But I'm not looking for a bargain; I'm looking for quality material, and Mrs. Adallah told me about a certain shop where I could find the best fabrics to make clothes with, so I'm headed there.

After a few locals point me in the right direction, I find it behind a few stalls. It's an open store without doors and windows, but it does have a roof. The lady behind the counter is folding some colorful fabric that awakens my inner magpie.

She follows my every movement as I search through the store, picking up various fabrics that I like. My hands can't help but touch every single one because texture is everything. And as I traipse through the store, my eyes can't help but catch some men arguing at a stall.

But I stop in my tracks the moment I notice the familiar clothes … that I saw at the club the evening I met Amir.

My eyes widen as I realize it's really him.

Again.

And this time, he's not wearing that white garment, but black pants and a dark blue shirt with a scarf around his mouth instead. Almost as though he's trying to blend in with the crowd of people again.

He grasps something from a lady and places it in the hands of the man. He scolds the woman, who seems to be crying, and then speaks to the manager again. They agree on something, and the man returns to business. After which, Amir turns his head back toward the woman, places his hand on her shoulder, and whispers into her ear.

A smile appears on her face, and she nods. Then she scurries off, and Amir covers his face with the same scarf I saw before.

That's when he glances my way, and our eyes momentarily lock.

Shocked, I grab the first thing I can find—a few long drapes of red fabric—and hide behind it.

Nothing will hide my obvious blush the moment he rips it away from my hands.

Shit.

Why now? Why is he here? And why do we always run into each other?

"Well, well, well, what do we have here?" he mumbles with a lopsided grin.

"Oh, brother …" I roll my eyes as I turn around and grab a random piece of cloth just so I can take my eyes off him and hide my embarrassment.

"You mean prince?" he muses, placing his hand on the fabric I'm touching. "But if you prefer brother, I can get used to that."

"Okay …?" I say, making a weird face before trying to grasp something else and turn around again.

Except he keeps following my every move, copying what I'm doing as if he's making fun of me.

"Why are you here again?" I ask, narrowing my eyes at him.

"Oh, I just happen to like going to the market."

"While pretending not to be a prince?"

He shrugs. "Maybe." His handsome smile follows, and it's hard not to smile back.

Goddamn him and his charms.

"I just don't like being followed."

"Right," I reply, trying to cut things off, but he won't let up.

"Plus, staying at the palace is boring."

"Oh, do tell," I say with a pinch of snark. I hope he won't throw me in jail. Probably not, but I shouldn't push my luck.

"Hey, it's not easy, you know. Being a prince."

Of course. Here we go.

"Really? Because girls aren't waiting in line for you? Because you have so much money and so little to spend it on?"

"No, that's not the point," he says, frowning. "And I don't have girls lining up for me."

"Sure about that? I just saw you whispering to another one back there," I say, gawking at the stall where I saw him.

"That lady was being harassed by the stall owner because she stole some jewelry," he says with a sudden serious face. "All I did was give the man his necklace back and give her some money so she could buy food with it."

"Food?" I bite my lip. "But—"

"Not everyone here has enough to get by," he says. "I just wanted to help. So I told her she could come to the palace and ask for Mrs. Adallah so she wouldn't have to resort to crime to pay for her food. That's all."

Wow.

That ... just blew me away.

I'm momentarily fazed. I don't know what to do or what to say other than stare. I feel like an idiot. I misjudged him, and now I feel bad for doing it. Damn.

"Oh ... that's really nice of you," I reply, licking my lips, wishing I had something better to say.

He shrugs and scratches the back of his neck. "It's what we're supposed to do."

I nod and continue picking up fabrics, trying not to make this any more uncomfortable than it already is. Maybe he really is a nice guy, deep down.

"So what are you doing?" he asks after a while.

"Buying fabric for the designs."

"Ooh, nice! See anything good yet?" He casually strolls behind me, not letting me out of his sight.

"I'm trying," I reply, hinting that I need to get to work.

"What about this?" He holds up a blue one with white lines on it, which would look horrible with what I have in mind.

I laugh. "God, no."

"Or this?" He holds up another one, this time a pure red one with tiny stars on it.

He clearly enjoys picking the worst ones just to see my reaction. That or he's really clueless about style. Either way, I'm not sure what he's going for or why he's even here.

I stop in my tracks, and say, "Look, I appreciate that you're trying to help me, but—"

He's suddenly right in front of me, waving a thin white fabric in front of my eyes that has bold black lines on it. "This one then."

I lower the fabric so I can look into his eyes. But I'm not prepared for the effect they have on me because it reminds me of when we kissed … *and* how we fucked almost immediately after that. Heat bubbles to the surface of my skin.

"What do you think?" he asks, raising a brow in such an arrogant way that I can't even look away.

I smirk as I touch the fabric. It's actually not even that bad. "You want this?"

He licks his lips. "Oh, yes …"

A shiver runs up and down my spine.

Why do I get the sense he's not talking about the fabric?

He lowers it farther, and says, "There's more that I want, but it wouldn't be appropriate to ask."

I'm completely stunned. Flabbergasted. My whole face turns red.

I immediately turn around and grab something else, something I don't need, a ribbon, but anything is good right now because it means I can use it as an escape.

"This will go perfect with that," I mutter, snatching the fabric away from him and then walking away to another shelf.

I don't know what it is about him that makes me so panicky. Maybe it's his looks, his gazes, or maybe it's the fact that he's a prince and I'm just a random girl from America trying to make her business work.

And this guy … he's jeopardizing it all, and for what?

"Where are you going?" he asks.

"Grabbing the things I need and then leaving."

"But we were just having fun."

I stop in my tracks right as he turns the corner toward me again. "I'm not here to play games."

"Who says I'm playing games? I'm dead serious," he says, approaching me.

He's got me cornered between two shelves now. Shit.

"I just want to talk."

"Why? What's so important?" I ask.

His tone is so smooth, it's hard not to completely hone in on his lips. "Well, for starters, I wanna know why you're doing your very best to avoid me."

I rub my lips together, trying to form a reply, but I have no clue what to say. I don't want to admit that I feel something when I'm around him—whatever it is that I'm feeling—because it just can't happen.

"I'm not," I lie.

"Yeah, you are," he says, coming even closer. He cocks his head and places a hand on the shelf just beside me. "Are you afraid of me?"

"Me? Afraid?" I snort. "Why would I be afraid?" Could my voice sound any more fake? I doubt it.

"Because of what I could do to you …" he says, his voice sultry. Almost addictive to listen to. Especially when he leans in to whisper, "*And* your body."

I hold my breath as I feel his breath near my ear.

"I know you want me to. I saw you looking." His lips almost touch my neck. I can't breathe. "You wish you had been in that bath with me."

I push him back, and say, "Stop being such a player."

"Player?" He frowns, confused.

"I'm not falling for your tricks again, dude," I say, placing a finger on his chest. "I'm not that easy." At least, not a second time.

"I didn't say you were," he replies. "But I'm not giving up either."

"Why? You have plenty of other girls you can seduce. They'd all die for a chance to date the prince. Go ask them," I say with a sigh, folding my arms. "I'm sure they're dying to be with a prince."

"You keep saying that, but it's not true." He shakes his head. "They only want me *because* I'm a prince. I don't want them. My father forces me to spend time with women, mostly the rich ones, but they're boring. I don't want any of that." He grabs my hand. "I'd rather spend time with you."

I don't know what to say or what to do. I'm frozen in place. And as he leans in again, I don't back away even though his lips are so close to mine I can almost taste them.

Suddenly, a blinding flash of light goes off in front of me.

I blink a couple of times and block my face with my hands.

There's someone behind Amir.

Another flash.

"Fuck," Amir hisses.

By the time I realize what's going on, Amir is already dragging me out of the store. "Run!"

Chapter 7

AMIR

Fuck. I didn't think they'd find me, but apparently, they did. Fucking paparazzi. Always following me around. Guess I'll need to find a different outfit to disguise my identity because this one obviously didn't work.

I drag her through the alleys, going as fast as possible to escape the photographer. I'm not sure he was alone, and I really don't want to make a scene right now. Especially when she's with me. And I'm sure they already caught a glimpse of something I didn't want anyone to see. Fuck.

I pull her along while she keeps asking questions. "Who was that? What's happening? Where are we going? What about my fabrics?"

"You can get them later," I growl. "We have to hide."

We enter an alley and weave through some tiny streets

until I finally reach the only place I know we can hide without anyone calling the media. A small home in the middle of the city tucked between two gigantic apartment buildings. I knock on the door but go inside immediately, not waiting for someone to open it. I already know I'm welcome anyway.

"Sorry for the sudden visit," I say as Saida gives me a surprising look. "Can we hide out here for a few?"

"Amir! It's been so long since I last saw you," she says, smiling. "Of course, you can. C'mon in." She beckons me to follow her to the back into the yard where I always played as a child. Oh, the memories of me and Faiz throwing mud at each other, playing catch, and falling into the pond. Those were good times.

Saida places her hand on my back and guides us outside. "Do you want something to drink?"

"Sure," I say. "But don't go through the trouble of making something fancy. We won't stay long." I don't want to bother her more than I already have.

"Oh, nonsense," she says, waving it off as if it's no big deal. "Stay as long as you like."

Her warmth brings a smile to my face. Time flies by so quickly.

She goes back inside and into the kitchen while Miss Maya keeps tugging my arm.

"Where are we?"

I smile. "An old friend's home. He's … no longer here, but his mom and I know each other well. I supported her when things were rough."

"Ahh … Is he …?" she mumbles, afraid to finish her question.

"He passed away," I answer as I grab two foldable chairs and place them side by side in front of the plastic table.

"I'm sorry for your loss," she replies, sucking on her bottom lip. "You two must've been close."

"Yeah. I used to come here a lot when I was little. Faiz and I were best buds. I hung out here whenever I was trying to hide from the paparazzi."

"Not much has changed then," she muses.

I love the smile that follows. It makes her shine.

"Sorry about what happened back there in that shop," I say, clearing my throat. "I didn't mean to yank you away from there, but if we didn't—"

"They'd try to take more photos, and your face would be in the tabloids," she interjects. "Got it."

"And yours," I add. "I didn't want to do that to you."

"Ah …" She nods, sitting down in the chair. "So that happens often?"

"Comes with being a prince, I guess," I say, sitting down too. "I do hate it, though."

"I can imagine. Do they ever leave you alone?"

"No. Why do you think I wear this when I go out?" I pat my clothes and smile at her, which makes her laugh.

"Maybe we should find you a better disguise next time. That fabric with the tiny stars on it would do the trick." She snorts. "Not that I can design anything right now."

"Right. The fabrics," I say, biting my lip as I look her directly in the eye. "I'll get it done."

"What?"

"The fabrics. Don't worry about it." I hold up my hand when she tries to open her mouth, saying, "Don't say no. Just let me fix it. I promise I will."

She leans back in the chair, and says, "All right. If you say so." She doesn't seem at ease, though.

"What's wrong?"

"I was hired by Mrs. Adallah. If she finds out what happened today—"

"She won't," I interrupt. "I promise your job is safe. I won't let her fire you over something like this. It's my fault, so I'll take the blame."

She nods a few times. "So is she okay with us busting in here?" she asks.

I laugh. "Yeah, she's used to it. This is still my go-to spot to hide from the press. They never discovered it."

"Aha … smart." She winks and smiles back, and her gaze drifts off to the pond in front of us. "So what now?"

As my eyes gloss over her body and follow her gaze toward the water, a devious grin spreads on my face. "How about a swim?"

"A swim?" She snorts. "You're joking, right?"

"No, c'mon," I say, grabbing her hand and pulling her out of the chair.

"But I don't have a swimsuit," she sputters.

"Who cares? Saida has towels. We can dry off after," I reply.

She tries to fight me, but I drag her closer and closer to the edge.

"But I don't—"

"Stop making excuses and let's just have fun," I say, laughing as she digs her heels in the sand.

Too late, though, because I can just about manage to push her into the water. A splash follows her loud squeal, and I jump in after her.

The cold water immediately wakes me up. God, I love this so much. I used to do this all the time with Faiz when I was still young. It's been years, and I honestly miss this. But I have to say, her being here with me makes up for it big time.

"My clothes!" she screams, making me laugh. "Everything is wet!"

"*Everything*?" I joke, raising a brow.

The glare she gives me is priceless. I don't know why, but I just love getting under her skin. The fire that blazes in her eyes is inextinguishable, and it sets a hunger ablaze inside me I didn't even know existed.

"You know what I mean," she says, folding her arms. "Are you having fun yet?"

"Oh, yes," I say, smirking like a motherfucker.

"Glad one of us is," she says. She frowns, but it won't stop the smile she's so desperately trying to hide from appearing on her face.

Suddenly, she splashes me with water. I blow out a big breath, rubbing my face while she's laughing hysterically. I love the sound of that.

Still, I can't help but throw some water right back at her, covering her too.

Now that we're on even ground, the fight only intensifies, and we both do our utmost best to get each other even wetter. But she's fierce and won't back down, and I'm gasping for air, begging for mercy.

"I give in!" I say. "I yield!"

She laughs and splashes the water onto my face a final time. "That's for throwing me in."

"I deserved that," I say. However, only now do I notice

just how close together we are in the pond. And just how sexy she looks with wet clothes sticking to her body, accentuating all her curves.

Instinct makes me wade toward her. I can't help myself. I want to push her buttons. I want to see her explode. And I want to touch her ... in every spot she keeps to herself.

I want it all.

***

Maya

One minute, we're dunking each other in the water, and the next, he's so close I can almost whisk the droplets from his skin. The water droplets roll down his face and chest, exposing the thick muscles underneath his thin shirt. Just looking at him makes me gulp with need.

I don't even know what I'm feeling right now except that I find it hard to resist touching him.
Apparently, I'm not the only one.

Before I've realized it, his hands have already snaked around my waist to the small of my back, pulling me close. I suck in a breath as his sultry eyes settle on mine with an intense gaze, one that could melt panties in the blink of an eye.

I can't look away, no matter how hard I try. Can't stop my body from gravitating toward him, despite my brain telling me no.

He's a prince. He's way out of my league. We're from

two different worlds. This couldn't ever—

Right then, his mouth crashes into mine.

Every thought, every worry instantly disappears.

Sparks run all the way through my body, filling me with a desire I didn't know I had. And I kiss him back.

His lips taste like sweetness and sin wrapped in a heavenly package. Everything I shouldn't crave, and everything I need at the same time.

He sucks on my bottom lip, and my mouth draws open as he forces his tongue inside, claiming my mouth as though it already belongs to him. I'm powerless to stop it. Defenseless against the onslaught of emotions and lust coursing through my veins.

Only when I hear someone giggle behind us do I come back to reality.

My eyes flash open only to find the lady who owns the house hiding her smile behind her hand. She caught us.

"I see you've already found a way to cool down," she says, sniggering.

My cheeks start to glow, but Amir doesn't even seem to notice she's interrupted us. All he can focus on is me.

However, a sudden sharp pain makes me shriek. I look around me.

The lady almost drops the two drinks she was carrying as she puts them on the table.

"What's wrong?" Amir asks, clutching my arms.

"My leg!" I squeal, trying to run past him while simultaneously kicking everywhere. "I think something just bit me!"

That's when I see it slither past us through the pond.

A snake.

Chapter 8

AMIR

I apologize to Mrs. Saida and immediately take Maya to the hospital. The poor woman only just managed to put some blankets around her before I lifted her off. We don't have any time to lose right now. This could be serious. Dangerous. Deadly.

We don't know what kind of snake it was. It could've been anything. And if it's venomous … I don't even want to think about what could happen then. In this country, the chances are very high, which is why I'm rushing her to a cab right now.

Even though my clothes are still soaking wet, I get in too and give the driver some cash. I don't care that he recognizes my face, and mumbles, "Your Hi-highness."

"Just drive," I say.

"Of course, Your Highness, sir!" he rambles, clearly flabbergasted that the prince just stepped into his cab. "Where to?" he asks.

"Hospital. As fast as you can."

"Yes, My Prince," he replies, immediately hitting the gas.

"I'll give you more cash if you get us there safely and without alerting the press."

"Got it."

As we race to the hospital, I ask her, "Where's the wound?"

She holds up her leg and points at the two marks.

I rip a piece off my clothing and wrap it around her leg. "Keep that on tight."

She nods, beads of sweat trickling down her forehead as the blood seeps through the compress.

I'm feeling anxious too. My heart is pounding in my chest, and I keep glaring out the window, wondering how much longer it's going to take. Every second is too long.

"Are we there yet?" I growl.

"Almost, Your Highness," the cabby answers.

"Go faster," I snap. I know I'm an asshole, but being nice isn't on my top list of priorities right now, knowing what just happened. She could be in serious pain … or worse.

Snake bites are deadly, but I'm not about to let her die. Not on my watch.

I've been through that once. It won't happen again.

When we finally get to the hospital, I immediately ask the ER for help. Showing them my passport is enough to speed things up. I know I'm not supposed to abuse my power as a prince, but I can't let this girl wait in line. Not when we don't know what bit her.

So they bring her to a private room and put her on the bed, immediately checking her over.

I sit in the chair next to her bed and wait until the doctors leave for a few blood tests. Meanwhile, she seems to have calmed down a lot. I haven't, though.

"Doctors say it's probably not venomous," she says, smiling. "Otherwise I would've felt something by now."

"We don't know for sure until the test results are back," I say, biting my nails.

She smiles and reaches for my hand. "It's okay."

"How are you so calm?" I ask. "You could …"

She shrugs. "I'm in good hands." Both our eyes shift toward our hands, which are clasped together. I gently caress her with my fingers, wishing I could do more.

"You look worried," she says.

I nod. "Snake bites … terrify me. It's what killed Faiz."

"Oh, I'm sorry. If I'd known, I wouldn't have—"

"It's okay," I interrupt, smiling. I don't want her to pity me. I want her to focus on her own health. It's far more important to me.

"I can't fix what happened to him. I can't bring him back, but I can take care of you," I say.

Her face turns strawberry red, and it's the most beautiful thing I've seen in a long while. Everything fades when she's around. This hospital. The fact that I'm a prince. Or that she's not even from Dakai. None of it matters anymore.

All I know is that I want to be close to her. Now. Tomorrow. Any day is fine. As long as I get to be in her vicinity.

I know our time is limited, and that she'll go back to her

country someday, but that doesn't mean we can't enjoy the time we have right now. And I intend to enjoy it to the fullest.

***

Maya

When the doctor comes back and brings the good news that it wasn't a venomous snake and that it was just a bite, I breathe a sigh of relief. They bandage my leg, and I thank them thoroughly for their hard work.

Amir hasn't left my side, and he's even helped me get out of bed and into a wheelchair. I never expected him to be this worried about me. He's really attentive to people's needs. Even though he's buttery smooth toward the nurses, chatting them up, he always follows up with a gentle touch to the arm and a compliment. It's not just to charm his way into people's hearts. I get the feeling he genuinely cares about the people. *His* people.

He's a prince, after all, and one day Dakai will probably be his.

And what am I? A random girl from America. I'm totally out of place here ... and totally out of line for kissing him.

What if the paparazzi find us again? Or worse ... his father?

I don't have to wait long to find out, though, because the staff are already on high alert, bouncing around the hospital as though there's a medical emergency.

Except there isn't.

The king has just arrived.

My jaw drops the moment I spot him and his entourage as they barge through the doors. Everyone stops their work and bows or greets him with great enthusiasm. People seem to honor him like some kind of god, or maybe they're terrified, but I have no way of knowing. They probably wouldn't ever tell a stranger what they really think. It could be dangerous.

But what's even more dangerous is the fact they're coming straight toward my room.

My eyes widen, and I clutch my wheelchair tight as if that will help me escape faster. Not that I'd ever get out of here without a reprimand or worse. They might even throw me in jail for what I did with the prince.

Oh God, I hope not.

Sweat rolls down my back as the bearded man approaches me, his stature and way of walking making me feel small and unimportant. Especially when he sets his gaze on me after glaring at Amir for just a second.

Amir suddenly places himself between me and his father, standing in front of me so I can't even see him look.

"Amir," his father barks. "What are you doing here?"

"Taking care of someone," Amir says, folding his arms.

"Who? This *girl?*" His father casually leans sideways to peek at me, but Amir follows his movements, blocking me from his sight again.

"She got injured."

"That is not your business to deal with," his father replies. "Have you any idea what kind of ruckus you've caused?"

Amir seems taken aback. "I apologize, Father, but the paparazzi were following us, so I had to act quickly."

"You brought this upon yourself the moment you stepped outside the palace wearing that ... that," he hisses, eyeing him like a hawk. "Whatever *that* is."

"They're just clothes," Amir replies.

"Why do you lower yourself so much?" his father gripes. "You are a prince. It's time you started acting like one."

"But I'm a human too, and I need fun too," Amir says, a bit defeated.

Without thinking about the consequences, I grasp his hand. I want him to know I'm here. He doesn't have to take on his father alone. And from the way he briefly glances over his shoulder at me, I know he can tell my intentions are sincere.

His father doesn't seem too pleased. "It's all over the newspapers ... you and *that girl* over there. What is she doing with you anyway? I should have her thrown in jail for how she's made you behave."

"Her name is Maya, and she's not made me do anything. This was all my choice. Leave her out of it," Amir growls. "And for your information, she was hired to design my clothes."

"A commoner? You're hanging out with a *commoner*?"

"She's not a commoner. She's American," Amir replies.

The guards accompanying the king seem on edge. "So? That only gives me more reasons to put her on a plane and send her back to wherever she came from."

Uh-oh. This is going downhill fast. Should I do something? But what?

"You can't just do whatever you please. You're a prince of the royal family. Our reputation is on the line. You have duties. Rules to follow."

"I'm sorry, Your Highness," I suddenly say, trying to push past Amir with my wheelchair. "It was not my intention to steal him away from the palace."

"Don't say a word, Maya," Amir interrupts.

"Indeed," his father says, snorting. "I didn't ask you for your opinion, girl."

"I am only here to fulfill my job, and that's it. I won't take up any more of your son's time, I promise," I continue.

Amir turns around and grabs my arms. "Stop. For both our sakes. Please."

The way he says the word "please" almost has me on my knees.

If I wasn't in this damn wheelchair.

Instead, I nod. I wish I could do more. He doesn't deserve this.

Amir turns toward his father again. "It's not her fault. I'm taking full responsibility."

"About time," his father says, turning around as he flicks his fingers. "Come. Time to go back to the palace where you belong."

Amir follows behind him, glancing at me over his shoulder with a smile. But as he leaves with his father, I realize I might not see him again. Ever.

Chapter 9

Maya

The wound in my leg healed within a day, so I'm back at work again. However, the lecture I got from Mrs. Adallah wasn't so pretty. Apparently, the king had spoken to her, expressing his distrust of me. He almost fired me on the spot, but Mrs. Adallah put in a good word for me, so luckily, I got to keep my job.

But it's not without caveats. I'm not supposed to talk to the prince anymore. At least, not unless it's business related. So I can make his clothes and show them to him, but that's it. I have to keep my mouth shut otherwise.

I guess I should be happy they're not sending me home. This is a big opportunity, and I don't want to ruin it. So I'll keep my head down from now on and focus on my work. No matter how hot he is or how delicious his kisses are, I have to stop thinking about him.

Too bad the moment I step into my workshop, I'm greeted by a gigantic bouquet.

And a whole stack of fabrics.

What the …?

Confused, I place my bag on the table and smell the lovely flowers. Tucked within is a card with gold letters engraved onto it.

Please forgive me for stealing your time yesterday. I hope the fabrics and flowers please you.

Amir

Please you. I can't stop reading those two words. And I can't stop the dirty images from appearing in my mind along with it too.

Crap.

I shake my head. I really have to stop doing this. And he needs to stop being so charming.

I give the flowers some water and then go through all the fabrics he bought for me. They're from that shop in the middle of town where we saw each other. He really did honor his promise.

Smiling, I pick up the ones I love the most and check them out. Bright purples, some with reds, a lot of white and black. Soft and velvety. Oh, yes … I can definitely work with these.

***

Days later

When I arrive at the palace, I go through the screening process and then go straight to Amir's room. The guards have already been alerted because they immediately let me in his room. Not without a stern look, of course, but I ignore it.

The room's empty. Well, except for all the luxurious furniture, lavish closets, carpets, drapery, and other things that belong to a prince.

But he's not here. Is he coming later, or did he forget?

Not that it matters. If he's not here, I can always show Mrs. Adallah the clothes I've created. Even though I'd much rather have him wear them first. I need to know if they fit. But maybe he'll be here later.

I place the big bag I brought on his desk and start unpacking, keeping the clothes neatly folded so they don't crinkle. I match the items and place them side by side, wondering what he'll think.

"Beautiful."

His sudden voice makes me squeal and jolt up and down. When I turn around, I immediately regret it. He's right in front of me … and only wearing a pair of tight swim trunks.

I shut my eyes, my face turning completely red. "Amir!" I say.

"What?" He laughs. "It's not like you haven't already seen it all."

"Jesus," I huff. "Put some clothes on."

"Gotcha," he says, sniggering as he grasps them from the desk. "These will do just fine."

I take a sneak peek when he's turned his back toward me and watch him put on the clothes I designed. I can't stop staring at the flexing of his muscles with every movement. He's right. The clothes do look beautiful on him. Then again … anything would with that body.

When he turns around again, it's hard not to drool.

"And? What do you think? Good?"

I nod. I don't even know what to say. He's gorgeous. And still totally a prince that I should not be thinking about in the way I am right now.

He smirks. "Love it. Exactly what I needed."

I smile. "Glad you like it. And thank you for the fabrics."

"No need to thank me," he says. "I told you I'd get it done. I always keep my promise."

He places his hand on my waist, pulling me close. "Did you like the flowers too?"

The seductive look in his eyes makes my head spin. "They were lovely. Thank you."

I spin on my heels and focus on the clothes I placed on the desk, trying not to get distracted by his coarse hands finding their way underneath my shirt. I'm melting into a puddle, but I can't allow this to happen. Not with everything that's at stake.

"Amir, we—"

"Shh," he interrupts, his hands snaking their way around my belly.

His lips press a gentle kiss on the back of my neck.

"You don't have to say a word."

And that's just it. I don't even know what to say. All I know is that this could put us both in danger. I could lose my job, and he ... well, his father could punish him, and I don't even wanna think about what he'd do to us if he found out.

"Let's continue where we left off ..." he whispers into my ear.

He gently coaxes me backward, away from the desk. His lips on my skin make me lose all sense of reality. Until I open my eyes again and realize we've only had him put on just one of my designs. He hasn't even touched the rest. This is what I came here for. What I was hired for. What if Mrs. Adallah comes in and sees us? It'd be the end of my time here. Or worse ... my entire career.

"Wait," I say, trying to pull away.

However, he holds me, refusing to let go. It makes me stumble backward into him, and he loses his footing too. I squeal as both of us fall, entangled together.

Not onto the floor ... but right into his bath.

I sputter and splash as I come up for air, the lukewarm water waking up my senses.

"Amir!" I shout as he was the one who dragged me in with him.

He laughs out loud, shaking his head, which makes droplets of water fly everywhere. "It's just water. Relax."

"The clothes!" I say, pointing out that he's still wearing them.

"A bit of water won't ruin them, right?" he muses, approaching me again.

I sigh and then sink into the water. I guess it's already

too late now. We're completely soaked.

"Sorry I dragged you in with me," he says, cornering me against the edge of the tub. "But you were the one who shoved me."

"I was trying to get away," I reply, licking my lips when I see the drops of water roll down his shirt. God, I wish the water didn't make it so clingy. I can see every inch of his muscles protruding through the fabric.

"Why? Afraid I'm going to kiss you again?" he murmurs, cocking his head.

He's so close now, I could almost taste him. Almost. I swallow hard.

"Because I want to," he whispers, inching closer and closer until our lips are just a breath away. "Really ... really badly."

Before I know it, he's already got his mouth locked onto mine.

Just like before in the pond, only this time I'm even more helpless to stop him. My mind goes on blank the moment his tongue parts my lips and claims mine. He circles around inside my mouth, taking me as if I always belonged to him.

He kisses me deep. Hard. In every way I always dreamed of being kissed.

And between each breath I take, he whispers sweet words that lay claim on my heart.

"You're so damn beautiful," he whispers. "Like the sun. I can't stop wanting to be in your presence."

He grasps my face with both hands, intensifying the kiss. It feels like I'm dreaming. Like I can't breathe.

I'm kissing a prince. A real prince. This can't be any

more outrageous or scandalous, yet I can't stop myself from kissing him back all the same.

One second is all I get to breathe, and I utter some words. "But we're supposed to be fitting clothes—"

"We can do that later," he murmurs against my lips.

His kisses grow more frantic with every passing second, and his hands find their way down my body, underneath my shirt. I'm overcome with a need I didn't know I had, wanting to feel his hands all over my body. My nipples peak as he rips off my shirt and tears off my bra, throwing them both into the water as if they mean nothing.

"Fuck ... do you know how long I've waited for this?" he groans, leaving sweet kisses everywhere.

I shake my head.

"Since day fucking one," he growls. "Back in the club. I've wanted to ravish you again and again ever since. Claim you, kiss you, lick you ... God, I want to do it all."

With rough hands, he grabs my waist and pulls me out of the water, propping me on the edge of the tub where he buries his face in my breasts. He grabs them and sucks hard, providing both with equal pleasure. If I wasn't already soaked, I just know my panties would be completely wet.

However, the pang of guilt still hits me right in the gut the moment I realize what's going to happen.

"But what if someone comes in?" I ask as he steals a kiss.

"No one enters without my permission, and I won't allow anyone in ... *or* out."

The way he says it makes my whole skin erupt into goose bumps.

The sound of his moans turns me on so much that I

actually spread my legs as he pushes himself between them. With two fingers, he tugs at my nipple, making it even harder while simultaneously licking the other. I writhe with pleasure, anticipating his next move as his hands travel down my body and peel down my pants until those too are gone.

My panties follow soon ... while he's still fully dressed.

Not that I have any time to think about it because he's got me right where he wants me. With his hand splayed on my belly, he pushes me down until my head reaches the floor while my legs are still in the water.

His face dips down between my legs.

I hold my breath. Is he really going to do what I think he's going to do?

"Hmm ... you've been dangling it in front of my eyes for so long," he murmurs, "I want to have a taste of that sweet pussy now."

His mouth settles between my legs, pressing a dirty kiss onto my skin. When I feel his tongue on my clit, I almost burst into flames.

He teases me with just the tip. Again and again, swaying back and forth, he licks me everywhere. And he does it with such a filthy grin that I feel like kissing and smacking him at the same time.

But that wouldn't be right ... he's the fucking prince of Dakai.

I'm being licked by the prince. And fuck me, does he know how to pleasure a woman.

I moan out loud as he circles around my clit, providing just enough pressure to make me want more, but not enough to push me over the edge. His fingers dig into my skin as he holds me, and I frantically grasp for his hair, wishing I could pull him closer.

The devilish look in his eyes shows he knows I'm close. So damn close ...

"Did you fantasize about me licking you like this, Maya?" he murmurs between lapping me up.

"Maybe," I say, a smirk appearing on my face. "Or maybe not."

"Don't lie. I know you did the moment you laid eyes on me, and I know you dreamed of being in this tub right along with me. And I know you've wished for my cock to be buried deep inside you again."

Why does he have to rub it in my face so much? Yes, I know he makes me horny. And I know I'm falling for him, but damn, he makes it so difficult. Does he want me to hate him? It's almost as if it gets him off.

"Fuck. You," I huff, trying not to let my face get completely red.

He sniggers and bites his lip. "I like it when you're feisty."

I knew it. I just know he loves to watch me get uncomfortable.

But I have no chance of fighting back, of fighting his tongue when it draws a line across my pussy. My body is helpless against the dirty tricks he's playing with my senses.

"And I like it when you're all wet for me," he groans, sucking my clit. "I wanna feel you come undone, Maya."

Before I know it, he's pushed a finger inside me, and I gasp as he swirls it around inside. Soon, another one is added, and I just about die from delight. Everything's coming at me all at once. The look in his eyes, the hunger, the flick of his tongue, the push of his fingers. It's too much.

With a loud moan, I explode all over him. Shockwave after shockwave ripple through my body, making me feel as if I'm on cloud nine.

It's been a long time since a man last made me come so good.

But I don't even get the time to let it wash over me because he immediately gets out of the water and lifts me into his arms. I squeal as he carries me away.

"Where are we going?" I ask, still dripping with water.

"My bed," he says with a smoking hot voice.

"But we're completely wet!" I say as he marches toward the other room.

A devious grin spreads on his lips, which makes me all hot and bothered again. "I'll dry you off … with my tongue."

Chapter 10

AMIR

I don't care what kind of excuses she comes up with; I'm taking her to my bed so I can fuck her brains out. I've waited long enough now, and I'm not interested in playing more games. I don't give a shit if my bed gets wet; it'll get cleaned up later. Nothing and I mean nothing's gonna get in my way of claiming her again.

"But what about—"

I put her down on the bed and immediately silence her with a kiss. I'm not going to change my mind. I don't care who finds out or what happens. All I know is that I want her, and that's the only thing that matters right now.

"Are you on the pill?" I ask her, my voice gravelly, almost untamable.

She nods, biting her bottom lip. "And clean."

"Good." I don't want anything between us this time. It's gonna be skin on skin.

With my hand, I push her down until she's flat on my bed. Her hands touch the silky sheets, caressing the fabric as though she's imagining it's me. I lick my lips, her body too tempting not to look at.

Then I slowly peel away the shirt she made, dropping it on the floor. Pants and underwear follow next, along with her eyes as my hard-on bounces up and down in front of her. I love the filthy sparkle in her eyes. I know she's been thinking about what it's like to feel me inside her … and I'm definitely gonna give it to her.

As she leans back, I crawl on top of her and bury my face in her neck, leaving a trail of kisses. Her gasps turn me on so much it makes my dick grow even harder against her thighs. I can't stop my hands from grasping her, slithering down to her ass, cupping it, and squeezing hard.

Her moans are like music to my ears, and in a moment of pure lust, I flip her over on her belly. I hush her squeal with a few kisses to the back of her neck, and her back arches against my dick as it settles between her legs. I grasp her firmly, spreading her and pushing the tip inside. Her mouth opens wide as I plunge into her deeply, letting her feel just how badly I want her.

"Can you feel how hard you make me?" I groan into her ears as I ravage her.

She can barely keep her eyes open as I thrust into her, so I grab a fistful of her hair and pull hard, making her head tilt back so I can kiss her neck.

"Mine," I growl into her ear.

She doesn't seem to mind. In fact, her pussy's only

getting wetter by the second. It makes it impossible for me to control myself, and I find myself thrusting harder and harder. Our bodies collide with passion; drops of sweat mixing with water as we struggle to resist our own needs. Her heat clashes with mine in equal fervor, her body trembling underneath mine as I fuck her raw. My fingers dive between her legs so I can fondle her again, wanting to feel every ounce of her explode before I do.

"Are you gonna come for me again?" I whisper into her ear.

She sucks in a breath as I bury myself deep inside her, waiting for her response. "Yes, fuck yes," she moans.

I finger her harder while also ramming into her, and I can tell from the way her eyes roll into the back of her head that she's close. Her pussy tightens around my dick, and I stop flicking her clit and give her butt a hard slap. The ripples that follow feel so goddamn good that I come too, howling out loud. And I fill her up to the brim with my cum.

But I'm not sated yet.

Pulling out, I flip her over again and keep rubbing my dick, wanting every last drop to land on her. I don't know why, but I feel the incredible urge to mark her as my own, so I do.

With one hand, I hold her legs open, digging my nails into her skin while I furiously jerk myself off with the other. She's panting, her hands firmly clenching the sheets as her orgasm subsides.

Just that look of utter pleasure in her eyes is enough to set me off again. "Fuck," I groan, overcome by my own lust.

Another jet of cum shoots from my cock, landing right

on top of her pussy, her belly, her tits. Nothing is spared, and I keep going until her entire body is covered.

When I'm sated, I swipe my dick on her pussy and shove it back in once more for good measure. I want her to know this is mine. She belongs to me now. Every … single … inch.

Panting, I lower myself on top of her again, pressing sweet kisses to her lips. I keep going until her lips part and that beautiful smile appears again. God, I could stare at that for days and never grow tired of it.

I just love the way she looks right now—naked, curled up underneath me, right where she belongs. With me. By my side.

I don't want her to go anywhere. I want her to stay. However long she can. Just for now. Or maybe forever. Would she? I don't think I've ever felt his way about a woman. I'd normally get them dressed as quickly as possible and hurry them out the back door before my father finds out I've been bringing girls to the palace again. Especially ones who aren't suitable for royalty, according to him.

But with Maya … it's different. She's not like the other girls. She didn't know I was a prince, and even when she did, she wanted nothing to do with me. She doesn't like me because I'm royalty; she likes me for me. Because we connect on a different level. Because we can't get enough of each other.

And I think she knows that too. I can see it in her eyes as I lie on top of her, leaving gentle kisses. I know she can feel it, our hearts beating against each other … already in sync.

"Stay with me," I whisper.

"What?" she mutters.

"You heard me," I say with a smirk, rubbing my nose against hers.

"Wait, what? No. We can't. I mean, I'm your designer. And you're a … prince." She almost swallows the last word as though she finds it hard to admit.

"So?" I reply, caressing her face. "I don't care. I want you."

Her cheeks glow red like a strawberry again. "You don't mean that."

"Why would I lie?" I say, frowning.

She pushes me off her and sits up, grasping the sheets to cover herself with. "I'm not a toy, Amir. Don't play with my heart."

"I'm not," I say, crawling up too, but she moves away when I do.

"Oh God." She buries her face between her hands. "What did we just do?"

"We had sex," I muse, laughing a little. "And it was fucking fantastic, just like last time."

"Great," she says, getting up from the bed. "I gave in. Again." She seems lost in her thoughts. "Stupid, stupid, Maya."

"Hey," I say, following her, "don't say that."

When I try to grab her, she spins on her heels. "No, you don't understand. I don't want to be just another one of your conquests."

"You're not."

"How many have you brought in before?"

"Why do you wanna know?"

"I don't," she says, shaking her head. "Never mind. The

point is, I never wanted to be one of them."

"You're not." I grab her hand. "You're special to me."

She rolls her eyes. "You probably say that to all of them."

"No, they'd be escorted out of here by now." Shit. That came out wrong.

She sighs. "Really?"

"I'm sorry, I don't mean it like that. What I mean is …" I pull her back toward the bed with both hands. "I like you. More than just any girl."

I place her down on the bed, and the sheets slowly drop back onto the bed too. The way she sucks on her bottom lip makes me want to kiss her again. But I know she'd probably avert her eyes if I did. She doesn't succumb to my wishes. Doesn't even care that I'm a prince. Maybe that's why I like her so much. She has a mind of her own, dreams, desires, and a whole business of her own.

She doesn't need me. That's why I'm so attracted to her.

And why she's so attracted to me … Because as we're sitting here on my soaked bed, completely naked, that spark between us is undeniable. So with my thumb and index finger, I reach for her face and kiss her again.

Right when someone barges into the room.

Her eyes burst open, and I release her chin from my grasp.

She squeals and covers herself with my sheets while my eyes draw toward the door in rage.

It's my father.

Chapter 11

AMIR

"What is the meaning of this?!" My father's voice echoes through the rooms. I didn't close the bedroom door. He can see us right from where he's standing near the door. And we're both completely naked.

Fuck.

I get up, shielding her from his attack. "Don't," I say, holding up my hand as he barges toward us.

"I told you not to bring those girls to the palace anymore!" he rages. "How dare you!"

"I'm a grown man, and I can do what I want," I reply, angry that the guards let him in even though I told them no one could disturb me—except Maya, of course. But apparently, they don't listen to my authority when my father intrudes. Goddammit.

"This is *my* palace. You may be a prince, but I'm still your father," he says, shoving his finger against my chest. "You should know better than to toy with random girls you picked off the street."

"She's not a random girl," I spit back. "Don't talk about her like that."

He cocks his head slightly, peeking over my shoulder. His eyes narrow. "*Her …*"

"Don't bring her into this," I say with a stern voice. "She has nothing to do with this."

"Then why is she sitting here naked on your bed, which is completely soaked?"

"It's my fault that it's wet. I fell into the bathtub and didn't dry off. Don't be angry with her, please." I position myself between her and him so he can't reach her.

"It's *my* choice. I brought her here."

"Isn't she your designer?" he growls.

I'm biting the inside of my cheeks to restrain myself. "Yes. And she has every right to be here."

"So now you're screwing the workers too?" he scoffs, laughing. "Amir, you need to stop playing around. This is no time to hook up with foreign girls."

"She isn't just a foreign girl. She's not just any girl to me, Father," I say. "That's what I've been trying to tell you all along, I like her. A lot."

"She is a foreigner. A commoner," he hisses, laying his gaze on her again. "You … I should have you thrown in jail."

"NO!" I growl back, pushing him away when he tries to get close.

She immediately bolts, still holding the sheets. "I'm

sorry. I'm so sorry," she mutters, grabbing her clothes. "This was a mistake."

"Maya, don't go," I say, walking up to her, completely ignoring my dad shouting at me from behind. "Stay, please."

"I can't," she says, shaking her head, tears welling up in her eyes.

I know he hurt her. No, *I* hurt her. It's because of me that she's in this position. I seduced her. Pulled her into my bed. Stripped her naked. And now my father found us ... It's all my fault. My burden to carry.

"I'm sorry," I say, sighing as I grab her hand. "Please, let me make it up—"

"I ... I ..." Her eyes shift back and forth between mine and my father's, and then she pulls her hand away. "I'm sorry, Amir."

And then she bolts through the doors, carrying all her stuff except the beautiful clothes she made for me.

***

Maya

Covered in tears and water, I clean myself up in the bathroom and put on my clothes before making a quick exit. I'm mortified of the people looking at me as if they're seeing a ghost. I know I look ridiculous, but at this point, I just want to get out of here fast. Screw looking decent. Screw saying goodbye. I'm out of here, and I don't ever wanna see this palace again.

As I make my way back to the hotel, the tears start to pour down my cheeks. I'm unable to keep them at bay, and I don't know why. Part of me is still in shock, I guess. That's what happens when the king finds you naked in bed with his son.

God, just thinking about it makes my whole face glow hot again.

I can't believe I let him seduce me like that again. Am I really that easy? Or does my heart really have a weakness for him?

I swallow away the lump in my throat when I think of his handsome face, telling myself I have to put it away and never think about it again. It was a one-time thing. Okay, a two-time thing, but it's never going to happen again. I'm never going to see him again.

I'm leaving, and that's that.

What's done is done. I can't change the past, but at least I can stop myself from hurting further.

So when I finally get back to my room, I quickly pack my bags and book a flight back home. I know it's only for the best. After all, if I don't leave by choice, who knows what could happen. His father might have me thrown in jail. I don't even wanna think about that option, so I'd better act fast and get out of here while I still can.

It doesn't take me long to get to the airport. I left the workshop and everything else as it was. I didn't bring anything other than what I came here with. I don't even care about the payment right now; I just want to get out of here.

So I get on the plane, determined not to let my heart cloud my judgment ever again. I knew it was a mistake to kiss him. I should've stopped myself before we went too far.

Now I'm having to sit down on a seat feeling completely gutted.

God, why does it feel like I'm leaving my heart behind?

***

AMIR

I spend an hour locked away in my room.

I don't want to speak to anyone. I don't want to see anyone. I just want to be left alone.

However, I can't stop fuming and pacing around my room, thinking of all the ways I could've done better, how I could've stopped her from leaving, how I could've ... *everything*!

It all just went by so quickly, and I never got a shot to repair what I broke. I didn't want to lose her. Didn't want to say goodbye.

But by the time I managed to escape my father's anger, she was long gone. Even the workshop was left as it was. It was like she was never even here to begin with.

And it pisses me off to no end. My father's so hell-bent on making me into what he thinks is the perfect son that he's losing me in the process. I don't care about being a prince. I don't care about this palace or all the riches.

All I want is her, and now she's gone. Disappeared. Forever, maybe.

And it's all because of him.

I'm left with a hole in my heart and a wish to scream my lungs out. So I do. Without regret, without any doubt, I release my rage on my father the moment he appears in my room again.

"This is your fucking fault!" I yell, pointing at him as he steps inside without knocking.

"How dare you raise your voice—"

"No, how dare *you* ruin this for me? Maya was the one girl I wanted to keep."

"Oh, please, she's just a foreigner who was here for work. That's it," he says, waving it away as though it's no big deal. But it is to me. It's time he finally understood. "When are you going to get over it? It's time you got back to business."

"You don't get it." I tap him on the chest. "You want me to become a prince. Someone people can admire. Someone fit for the throne. Yet you don't even let me make my own decisions. You think you need to control me, but you're pushing me further and further away."

"A prince should care more about his country than himself," he says.

"Maybe I don't wanna be a prince," I say, pacing around the room. "Ever think about that?"

"You don't have a choice," he says.

"Except I do. I could walk out of here tomorrow and never come back."

His face turns dark, like thunder and lightning. "You wouldn't."

"Don't tempt me," I say, clenching my fist. "Because I really am thinking about it."

"Why?" he asks, approaching me, but I look away. "Over some girl? You've lost your mind."

"No …" I grasp the clothes she made and hold on to

them, smelling them, knowing they were in her hands. They still carry her scent. I wish I could smell it one more time.

"I've lost my heart."

The gravity of it all sinks in like a stone, and I feel like I can barely breathe when I look at the mess that's left.

"You've fallen in love?" he asks. "With a commoner? That's not possible, you're—"

"A prince. I know."

"Exactly."

"Then I don't want to be a prince," I say, gazing at him over my shoulder.

"What did you say?" He frowns.

"You heard me," I say, standing my ground. "If I can't have her, it's not worth it."

"Nonsense. There are plenty of other actual royal girls available."

"I don't want them. I want her. End of story."

"And what if I don't agree?" He places his hands against his side.

"Then I'll quit."

"Quit what?" He scoffs. "Being a prince?"

I nod. "I don't care."

"You'll lose your right to the throne," he says. "The palace. The money. Everything."

I shrug. "It means nothing if I can't choose who to love."

His lips part, but there's no response. I know he can see the look on my face. I mean it for real this time. No joke. This is it.

"You're willing to risk everything for *that* girl?" he asks.

I nod. "I told you, she's not just any girl. At least … not

to me." I sigh. "I want her. Only her."

"So you're dismissing all the potential royal ladies waiting for you to make a choice?" he asks.

"They only want me so they can be queen." I scoff.

He frowns. "You don't know that."

"The ones you've made me date so far have. And that girl, Maya … she doesn't want me because I'm a prince. She just likes me for who I am." I approach my dad. "And having her in my life was the best thing that's happened to me in years."

Father sighs out loud, visibly disappointed. And I get it. His son isn't who he thought he'd be. Maybe it's only right that I give everything up. I haven't exactly proven myself to be a great future king.

So I turn around and march for the door.

"Where are you going, Amir?" he asks.

I'm tired of letting him decide for me. This time, I'm making my own decision. "To find her."

"And do what exactly?"

"Win her back." I'm determined. I won't let him persuade me to stay or ignore my feelings for her. It's too late for that. It's time I made the right choice.

"She's probably already gone," he says.

"I don't care. I'll chase her if I have to."

"Out of the country?" My father gasps.

I shrug as I open the door. "So be it. One way or another, I'm gonna get her back."

Knowing her, she'll have already packed her bags, gone back to her hotel, and booked her flight home. Maybe I'm too late, but that won't stop me from flying after her.

Nothing will stop me from being near her. Nothing.

Chapter 12

Maya

As I'm waiting for the plane to take off, the crew are bustling back and forth between the seats, trying to get everyone's luggage in place.

However, a particular disturbance at the front makes me grow leery. I peek over the seats in front of me, trying to catch a whiff of what's going on. People are holding up the line as they're getting on, most of them talking amongst each other and smiling.

I wonder what's going on.

The commotion keeps the crew busy as they try to delegate the passengers and tell everyone to remain seated. I peer through the windows to try to catch a glimpse, only to find even the people in the terminal are completely taken by what's going on.

That's when I spot it. The small cart skirting through the terminal, sirens on, with lots of people on board. They're headed straight for the gate, but people around them are taking pictures of the spectacle.

Only when the cart disappears do I realize that it was *my* gate they were headed straight through.

And someone just called out my name.

"Is there a person named Maya on board?" one of the crew members from the front calls out.

I get up and wave awkwardly. "That's me."

"Can you come to the front of the plane, please?"

Everyone's looking at me now, and I feel embarrassed by the sheer volume of eyes pinned at my back. But I persist as I head to the front, clutching my bags, wondering what the hell is going on.

I don't have to wait long to find out.

At the entrance to the plane, Amir is waiting with a giant bouquet in his hand and a smile on his face that could make any girl melt into a puddle.

My bags instantly drop from my hands.

"Amir?" I mutter.

He grins. "In the flesh."

I'm completely dumbstruck. "How?"

"I got Mrs. Adallah to talk. Pulled some strings at the airport and security. There's not a lot people won't do for the prince," he says with a smug smile.

My jaw is still practically on the floor. "But why?"

He comes toward me and stops right in front of me. "Because I want you," he says.

"But I ... I ..." I don't even know what to say. The fact

that he came all the way here just to beg me to stay has me completely baffled.

"I don't care what I have to do. If you want me to go on that plane with you, I'll do it. I'll give up the right to ever become king."

The people around us cover their mouths in shock.

"Amir, no, don't say that. This is important for you," I say.

"Not as important as this," he says, grabbing my hand. "I've finally found what I really need. What I want. And I don't wanna lose that."

"But we've only known each other for a few days …"

"All the more reason to give this a chance," he says. "I've known it since I first met you; there is something special between us that I can't just ignore. I need to know what it is. I need you with me."

"But—"

"Say you'll stay, please." His voice makes me question everything I thought I was doing.

I thought I was making the right decision by getting on this plane and never coming back here, but now that I've looked him in the eyes, it's so hard. Nothing has ever been this hard.

"If not, let me come with you," he says, smiling as he glances over his shoulder at a bunch of suitcases stacked up. "I brought some things, just in case."

I laugh. "I'm amazed. Is there anything you didn't already think of?"

"Well …" he says, licking his lips as he hands the bouquet to an assistant to hold while he talks to me. "The one thing I forgot was to stand up to my father. He hurt you, and I'm sorry that happened. Please forgive me."

I rub my lips together, fighting the tears as he goes on his knees right in front of me.

"Amir, get up," I hiss between my teeth as everyone around us starts gossiping out loud. "We're making a scene."

His dreamy eyes are locked on mine. "I don't care. Let them talk."

"But what about your father?" I ask.

"I told him the same thing. I don't care about being part of a royal family if I can't have what makes me happy, and right now, that's you."

"But you'll throw away your right to the throne," I respond, worried he might actually do that. I'm just … me. I'm not worth giving up his entire future for. Especially as a prince.

"I'd rather do that than throw away my only shot at a happy life with you."

The beaming smile on his face makes the tears roll down my cheeks. I can't fight them anymore. I don't even want to. No one has ever done anything like this for me before. It's like a fairy-tale dream come true.

"And you think your father would accept that?" I ask. "Would he accept me?"

"Once he realizes this is the only way, and that I won't let him decide for me, I'm sure he will. He was never mad at you; he was mad at me for choosing differently. But I know he'll come to his senses. Just as I did when I saw you run. I knew then that I never want to see you leave that way ever again."

I frown, still worried about all the things that could happen if I stay. What about my life back home? My family and friends? My job?

I gaze over my shoulder at the plane and everything I'd be leaving behind if I said yes.

"If you're worried about your home, I can bring your family here too. Anyone you want for as long as you need."

"You'd do that for me?" I ask, wiping the tears away. It's as though he can read my mind.

"Yes, because I love you."

My eyes widen, and my heart skips a beat.

Love. Did he actually just say that?

"What?" I mutter.

The smile on his face almost seems permanent. He's unafraid to admit his feelings for me and wants the world to know. "You heard me. I know what I want, and what I want is you. I'm not going to deny what I feel in my heart. Even if it's quick. Even if it's outrageous and pisses everyone around me off, including you."

I laugh at his comment because it's true, but it makes him adorable too.

"I don't care what it takes; I wanna make you happy," he says, and I can tell from his voice he means every word.

Still, the voices in the back of my head can't seem to shut up. "But what about my work, and—"

"There are plenty of customers waiting in line. I've looked at your popularity, and it's not just people in America who want your clothes. You're famous, Maya. And don't try to hide it from me."

I snort, shaking my head, but his compliments make it hard for me to reply without my face turning into a strawberry.

"I'll have the workshop upgraded, and any materials you

need will be provided. We'll ship them from abroad if we have to, and anything else to make your business flourish."

"But you're a prince, and I'm—"

"Perfect for me. In every way," he interrupts, grabbing both my hands now. "Say you'll stay. For now. As long as you want."

I raise a brow. "You've really thought this through, haven't you?"

"Damn right, I have." The smug look on his face makes my heart do a little spin even though the people around us all seem shocked he'd go through all this trouble just for me.

But that's just it … to him, I'm more than just that girl from America. I'm more than just his designer.

We had more than just fun. There's a connection between us, something powerful I can't explain, but it draws me toward him just as much as he's clinging onto me.

As I spent all this time at the airport, I was hoping, praying he'd come to get me.

And here he is to fight for me. How can I not say yes?

So I do. "Yes," I say. "I'll stay."

I'm deciding here and now I'm going to give it a shot. I owe it to my heart to stop waiting around for the right guy. This guy … he's the one I want right now, and I don't give a damn if that means giving up my life back home because life's all about risks and taking chances.

And I choose this path because it isn't a coincidence that we met. *We* aren't a coincidence.

So I don't stop nodding until it finally sinks in. He gets up from the floor and wraps me in his arms, twirling me around as he hugs me tight. The people around us erupt into cheers.

And for a minute, I even forget all the stares surrounding us as Amir plants his lips on mine and seals the deal.

Epilogue

Maya

Within a few weeks, I've already been relocated into the palace. I fought tooth and nail to have my own place to live, but his father actually wouldn't have it. Even though he was quite wary of me at first, he seems to have grown fond of me over the weeks. Apparently, I have a calming effect on his son, which has turned him from a playboy into a sophisticated prince. The clothing probably helped that image along too, though I'm not gonna take all the credit. Amir has been such a gentleman that it's amazing. Not just to me, but to the staff and the people in the country too. He continues to attend charity events, helping as much as he can and giving the people as much as he can give.

His father wasn't happy with it at first, but when he saw

the effect it had on his people, he's been participating too, which surprised me quite a bit. The man has made a U-turn in terms of engagement with both his subjects and me. And I couldn't be happier because it's made the transition to living in Dakai much easier for me when I can actually get along with my potential father-in-law.

Just thinking about it still makes my heart race. As if I could actually become Amir's wife one day. An actual princess. But I have to rein in those thoughts. I don't wanna go too fast. I wanna take things slowly and see where they go. My business and getting to really know Amir come first right now.

That, and my family, who are coming over next weekend to see me, along with a couple of my friends. Even my cousin Lesley who couldn't wait to tell me all about her adventures at her new dream job. I was so jealous when she first brought up the company she worked for, but I won't say that now.

Still, my family were very supportive of me when I told them I was staying here to pursue my dreams, and I even told them about Amir and how he's a prince. They were shocked, at first, just as I was, but after talking to them on the phone a few times, they seem to have accepted the idea of me being with him. I mean, he's still just a man, like anyone else … only royalty.

I'm so excited for them to come over, and it feels like my smile is permanently plastered to my face while I'm sewing together a dress I made that I'll wear while they're here.

"What are you grinning at?" Amir asks as he peeks over my shoulder.

"Oh, I'm just excited about my parents visiting," I answer, and I hold up the dress. "What do you think? Good?"

He smiles broadly. "Beautiful. Just like you." He places a soft, delicate kiss on the back of my neck, and whispers, "I can't wait to see you wear it."

I don't know why, but everything he says sounds so erotically charged. Or maybe that's just the sparks flying between us whenever we're close.

Because I have to admit, I'm having a hard time staying away from the palace or even his room. I can't help but gravitate toward him constantly. My body and heart have already decided they want to be close to him, and my mind is still trying to adjust.

"Hmm ..." Amir groans in my ear as he places another seductive kiss just below. "You smell so good."

"New perfume," I say, giggling when he places another kiss and adds a lick too. "What are you doing?"

"Isn't it obvious?" he muses, still kissing my neck, making goose bumps scatter on my skin. "I always wanna do dirty things to you, Maya."

"What? You're thinking about *that* right now?" I ask, placing down the dress.

"Yes, right now," he says, sucking on my earlobe. "And pretty much every other minute of the day."

I'm having a hard time concentrating. "But we have a lot of work to do. Preparations to make."

"It can wait ... *I* can't."

Amir's hands are on my breasts now, fondling them and pinching my nipples until I let out a slight squeal. "Tell me you don't like it."

"Just because I do, doesn't mean we should—"

He grins against my skin. "When has that ever stopped us? Last I checked, that's exactly how we found each other."

"How we got into this mess, you mean?" I say jokingly.

"And how we're gonna make an even dirtier mess," he whispers, pulling me up from my seat. "C'mon."

He tags me along back into the room that has the big tub all while keeping his mouth on mine. I only get a couple of seconds to breathe while his scorching mouth is everywhere. On my neck, my cheeks, and even my collarbones.

He tears off my shirt with no trouble, and my bra follows quickly. I pull off his shirt too, chucking it to the floor. I struggle not to trip over the clothes as he's kissing me fast and furiously, turning my brain to mush.

"Fuck, I want you so badly," he murmurs against my swollen lips, his fingers shoving down my skirt along with my panties. "I've been dying to get a break from all this work."

"Work? You?" I snort. "That's a new one."

"Hey, don't pretend you didn't see me work my ass off at that local soup kitchen," he says, turning his back toward me to turn the hot water on in the tub.

"I was watching something else," I say, and I quickly slap his butt when he's not looking.

He gasps and throws me a wicked glance over his shoulder. "Oh, you're in trouble now."

When he picks me up, I try to shriek, but before I know it, I've already been thrown into the water. He jumps in right after me even though he still has his pants on. But of course, he doesn't care. He never does. That's why I like him so much. He makes life fun and exciting. Like one big roller coaster I don't wanna get off.

***

AMIR

I pin her to the tub walls and kiss her as hard as I can. I don't know why, but I have the incredible urge to show her just how much I love her. How badly I want her to be mine. So I do it with my mouth and my tongue in all the right places, making her moan out loud. The sounds she makes get my cock hard, and I can't stop myself from groping her everywhere.

Still, I don't want her to be mad at me for interrupting her during work. I know how fussy she gets about it; how important it is to her. And I don't wanna make her feel like I'm only interested in her body, so I pull back. I bite my lip, and say, "Damn, I can never get used to how good you taste."

She giggles and rubs her lips together, trying to hide her grin, but it won't work on me.

"You said the same thing about something else," she murmurs.

"And I meant it," I reply, pulling myself up on the edge of the tub.

"Hey, where are you going?" she says, grabbing my leg.

"Just gonna sit here on the edge," I explain when she gives me a puzzled look. "I know you didn't wanna get in the tub with me, so I'm gonna let you go now. I don't wanna be the bad guy and keep you away from your work."

"You? The bad guy?" She snorts. "And who says I wanna work?" she muses, positioning herself between my legs. Her hands drift up my thighs, making it even harder for me to will my cock to go down. "Maybe I wanna do something else …"

"Hmm … You're only saying that because I want to," I say, leaning over to kiss her on the forehead. Because fuck me, I definitely want her right there.

"Maybe … or maybe not," she taunts, eyeing my cock right through my pants.

Before I know it, she's already hooked her fingers around the waistband and pulled both my pants and my underwear down. She throws them away and grabs my length with both hands, making it bob up and down.

"Whoa, you're excited," I say, leaning back with my hands flat on the floor.

"That's what you get when you throw yourself at me." She starts rubbing me, slowly at first, making me painfully aware of how badly I want her. And how bad I am at resisting the urge.

"Hmm … I'll remember that," I muse with a smug smile as I close my eyes.

"As if you weren't doing it to get laid," she murmurs, and her mouth sinks over my cock.

A gasp leaves my mouth, and I close my eyes. She knows just how to suck, licking my length all the way while applying ample pressure. It makes me want to shove her down all the way, but I have to restrain myself. I don't wanna scare her.

"Fuck, that feels good," I groan as she wraps her tongue

around my cock and sucks hard.

"I thought it was time to return the favor," she whispers as her lips circle the tip.

I moan out loud when she dives right back in again, bringing it down all the way.

Damn, this girl knows how to give head. As if it couldn't get any more perfect.

My fingers instinctively reach for her hair as I'm unable to stop myself from wanting to bury myself deep inside her throat. The noises she makes are such a turn-on, my balls tighten and the veins in my cock bulge with excitement.

Every few licks, she goes so deep, the tip hits the back of her throat. My whole body tenses as she works me from top to bottom. It's as though she wants me to come. And fuck me, am I ready.

"Fuck, I'm gonna come," I say.

"Fuck yes," she moans.

Her filth sets me off, and I shoot my load all the way into the back of her throat, covering her tongue too. The stream feels like it never ends, but she keeps swallowing it all.

By the time I'm fully sated and my dick is flaccid, she lets go with a gleeful smile on her face. She swallowed it all.

Fuck me. What a girl.

I bend over and grasp her face. "God, I fucking love you." I kiss her full on the lips, not afraid to show her just how good she makes me feel.

"*You're only saying that because I want you to,*" she replies, winking. Of course, she'd use my own words against me. Naughty girl.

So I reply, "You wish that was the case. But you're stuck

with me now, Maya. This prince isn't letting his princess off the hook, no matter what she does."

She licks her lips as she responds, "Good, because it's my turn now, and I want that dirty mouth all to myself."

THANK YOU FOR READING!

Thank you so much for reading! I hope you enjoyed the story!

For updates about upcoming books, please visit my website, www.clarissawild.com or sign up for my newsletter here: www.bit.ly/clarissanewsletter

I'd love to talk to you! You can find me on Facebook: www.facebook.com/ClarissaWildAuthor, make sure to click LIKE. You can also join the Fan Club: www.facebook.com/groups/FanClubClarissaWild/ and talk with other readers!

Enjoyed this book? You could really help out by leaving a review on Amazon and Goodreads. Thank you!

ALSO BY CLARISSA WILD

Dark Romance
Delirious Series
Killer & Stalker
Mr. X
Twenty-One
Ultimate Sin
VIKTOR
Indecent Games Series
FATHER
CAGED & LOCKED & CHASED & BRANDED & HANGED

New Adult Romance
Fierce Series
Blissful Series
Ruin

Erotic Romance
The Billionaire's Bet Series
Enflamed Series
Unprofessional Bad Boys Series
Hotel O

Visit Clarissa Wild's website for current titles.
www.clarissawild.com

ABOUT THE AUTHOR

Clarissa Wild is a New York Times & USA Today Bestselling author with ASD (Asperger's Syndrome), who was born and raised in the Netherlands. She loves to write Dark Romance and Contemporary Romance novels featuring dangerous men and feisty women. Her other loves include her hilarious husband, her cutie pie son, her two crazy but cute dogs, and her ninja cat that sometimes thinks he's a dog too. In her free time, she enjoys watching all sorts of movies, playing video games, and cooking up some delicious meals.

Want to be informed of new releases and special offers? Sign up for Clarissa Wild's newsletter on her website www.clarissawild.com

Visit Clarissa Wild on Amazon for current titles.

Printed in Dunstable, United Kingdom